Lord Rivington's Lady

Lord Rivington's Lady

by Eileen Jackson

WALKER AND COMPANY
NEW YORK

y

First published in the United States of America in 1976
by the Walker Publishing Company, Inc.

Published simultaneously in Canada
by Fitzhenry & Whiteside, Limited, Toronto.

ISBN: 0-8027-0533-2

Library of Congress Catalog Card Number: 75-40762

Printed in the United States of America.

Book design by Robert Bartosiewicz

10 9 8 7 6 5 4 3 2 1

CHAPTER 1

At the sounds of movement in the trees across the stream the two young women paused. " 'Tis a poacher," whispered the taller girl. 'If he sees us, he'll kill us, for sure."

"Nonsense!" her companion replied in a low, calm voice. "In any case, he'll not know we are here if you can keep your foolish teeth from chattering so loud."

In spite of her brave words, Georgina's face, naturally pale, grew a shade paler. Since the harsh act against poachers had passed seven years ago in 1803 many a man had hanged by his neck, kicking his life away simply for trying to fill the stomachs of his family—and who could blame anyone for trying to close the mouths of witnesses? A man could die but once.

The sounds came nearer, and the two girls shrank back. Then the smaller laughed softly. "What a bother we make of nothing, Eliza. It will be your father about his duties."

"No, miss, father's ill of a fever today and no one else would venture here, knowing his reputation as a gamekeeper."

No one but her foolish young mistress. They should be at

[1]

home, where a young lady of rank like Miss Georgina ought to be on a February day that was so cold that the flesh shrivelled on the bones. And Eliza could be in the kitchen kept warm and cosy from the heat of the great cooking range, instead of having to turn out to help carry the heavy basket of medicinal mixtures and victuals to villagers so full of poverty and disease they were not, in Eliza's opinion, worth the bother.

After listening intently Georgina began to walk again along the deeply rutted frozen path through the woods, picking her way carefully in the afternoon gloom.

"Why did you not tell me your father was ill, Eliza? When we return, I will make him a fever-reducing potion, and you shall carry it to him."

"Thank you, miss," muttered Eliza, hard put to keep a civil tongue and cursing the impulse which had led her to lie, but afraid to refuse the offer because her mistress would put down any hesitation to fear of the fever and insist on walking herself to the gamekeeper's cottage with the medication.

And Eliza knew that her father was even now sitting in the back parlour of the inn, bargaining with a passing higler over the price of the hares he had taken from the land which he was employed to protect. She had no wish to see her father dangling from a gallows, though if she had taken the trouble to study Miss Georgina, she would have known that her mistress would never help to enforce a law she believed cruel and unjust.

But Eliza's eyes saw only her own misfortunes; her ears heard only her own laments. She had gone to work for the Havards with her head full of ideas put there by her cousin Nancy, who was in service in London. She had notions of servants' tables properly divided by rank; of food so rich the stomach needed medicinal potions to allay the pangs of overindulgence; of cast-off gowns worn by the maids to impress the young footmen with which every house was supplied.

Reality was different. Of course she had heard the rumours that the once wealthy Havards were short of money since the late Mr. Havard had squandered his fortune and that of his first wife in gaming houses, but she had ignored such talk. Any family who lived in a dwelling the size of Havard Hall must be rich, and to her the economies practised and preached by Miss Georgina were a sign of meanness not thrift. Only poor folk like herself needed to count pennies.

She grinned behind her mistress's back. Sometimes the table at home boasted better fare than that of the Havards, when her father had diverted a plump hare or bird to his own cooking pot.

They had reached the boundary hedge of their neighbour's land, where growth was sparse and the stream which meandered through both estates was narrow with stepping stones. By crossing here they could take a short cut and reenter the Havard estates by a small bridge nearer the Hall. The stream at this point ran too fast for ice to have formed, but the stones were slippery and several times the girls clung together to retain their balance. They had almost reached the opposite bank when a large black dog raced through the trees before them and barking explosively leapt into the water, sending icy droplets over them.

Georgina shouted, "Quiet, sir!" as Eliza shrieked, clutched her mistress convulsively and overbalanced, dragging them both into the ankle-deep, icy mud at the edge of the stream.

Georgina dragged herself and the maid from the clinging slime and up the bank, where she stamped her feet, which shook off some of the mud and helped to relieve her feelings about the idiotic behaviour of the servant.

The barking dog leapt around them, and Eliza cried, "Let's go back, miss. That's a nasty brute. He'll attack us for sure."

"Eliza, you are without doubt an exceedingly silly crea-

ture. Can you not see that the animal is a puppy? His barks
are meant for greeting, and his tail is wagging. Here, sir,
come here!"

The dog bounded to her and lay across her feet, revelling
in her soft caress and panting joyfully. "I wonder where you
belong; you are no village cur," she murmured, and he
licked her hand at this appreciation of his worth.

A shrill whistle sounded and a voice cried, "Here, boy.
Here!" A moment later the owner of the voice appeared and
stood regarding the tableau. He was tall, over six feet Georgina judged as he approached them at a lithe saunter. His
movements gave an impression of athletic prowess, and his
shoulders were broad beneath his dark country garb. Thick
black curls sprang from a head left bare in defiance of the
biting wind, and grey eyes bored into Georgina's in an inso-
lent way which caused her to tremble in untypical feminine
weakness.

His first words drowned her momentary lapse in fury.
"Remove your hand from my dog," he commanded in a
voice which sounded lazy, but carried the unmistakable
tones of one who was used to instant obedience.

Perversely, Georgina continued to fondle the dog for several seconds before she rose. The man looked her slowly up
and down, taking in her plain wool gown and homespun
cloak. " 'Tis a pity your mistress cannot teach you a quicker
compliance with the orders of your betters," he drawled.

Astonishment left Georgina speechless as he turned his attention to Eliza, who was open-mouthed at her mistress's apparent acceptance of such a set-down. In contrast to Georgina, whose skin was pinched with cold, she had a rosy
bloom and tendrils of yellow hair escaped from her hood and
curled saucily above her slanting blue eyes.

He showed his admiration as he walked forward and
chucked her under the chin. "Very pretty, upon my word.
Tell me, are you kitchen wenches, or does your work take
you to the upper chambers? I've not noticed you around
Kennerley."

Eliza, who had begun to simper, gasped and let her mouth fall open. "You look remarkably like a fish," he grinned. "Don't you know what you do?"

Georgina spoke briefly. "We do not reside on these estates, and I am no servant, sir."

His eyebrows rose at her cultured accent. "No, you're no skivvy. What capacity do you fill, I wonder? Ladies' maid? No! Ah, I have it! A governess. A poor unfortunate engaged to impart information to unappreciative children." His eyes flickered over her once more, and she felt herself begin to shake as he continued, "It is to be hoped you teach your charges better manners than you have learned for yourself."

"Come, Eliza," grated Georgina, "it grows late."

She approached the man on the narrow path, but he made no move so, clenching her teeth, she tried to edge past him. He put out a hand and held her in a grip which was gentle, yet held the promise of steel. "Hold hard. If you do not work on these estates, then you are trespassing. What is your business here?"

Eliza, after a brief glance at her mistress's face, answered hastily, "We . . . we are at Havard Hall, if you please, sir. This is a short cut home. The old lord gave his permission for us to use it—before he died, that is, and I . . . I don't think the new young lord will mind."

"Have you asked him?"

His words answered Eliza, but his face was turned toward Georgina, whose cheeks held two vivid spots of colour. "Take your hand from my arm," she demanded.

"I repeat, have you asked him?"

"No, sir, we have not."

His wolfish grin showed strong white teeth. His eyes held a malicious gleam. "By right I should haul you before my host and let him deal with you as trespassers, but I've decided to be lenient. You may pass today, but remember in future to take the long way back—or beg leave from the owner of these estates to use his path."

Georgina jerked her arm from his grasp and almost ran

past him into the trees, followed by Eliza. In her rush to escape the stranger's hateful attentions Georgina mistook the way; in the gloom she raced along a path with which she was unfamiliar.

She found it necessary to watch for branches which slapped at her face, then she tripped over a root and stumbled into a briar bush, where Eliza joined her with a shriek. The maid's frantic struggles were embedding thorns more deeply into their skirts, and her loud cries infuriated her mistress.

"Idiot!" Georgina hissed. "If you keep up that caterwauling, that horrible creature will be upon us once more."

"Too late for caution, I fear; he already sees our predicament."

Georgina looked round into the mocking eyes of the stranger, who swept her a low bow. "Allow me to help you."

She shot him a look of loathing. "We do not need your assistance, sir."

"On the contrary. How could any gentleman leave two females in such dire need?"

Georgina worked desperately to disentangle herself, but succeeded only in scratching her wrist deeply.

The man smiled. "You see, you need me more than you know."

With slow deliberation he turned first to Eliza and released her before contemplating Georgina. Her anguished efforts had twisted her skirts in the thorns, and it took a great deal of work on the man's part to help her. She kept her eyes down and saw how deftly his hands tugged at the offending briars. Her lip curled as she saw their soft whiteness, then she remembered again the feel of those hands and the strong grip which belied their looks.

He pulled her cloak tightly about her body and almost lifted her back onto the path. No wonder he had taken her for an inferior—her garb was plainer than her maid's. How could he know that it suited her work to dress simply?

They stood close together on the frozen path, he still holding her cloak firmly about her. She felt her skin flush with rage; her eyes shone with unshed tears of chagrin. Georgina had no illusions about her appearance. Her looking glass told her she was not pretty. It said that her complexion was pale, her brown hair held a natural curl, and that her eyes were hazel.

She had no way of knowing that reflections can lie and that there were occasions when her indomitable spirit shone through her eyes, making them luminous; that emotion brought a glow of delicate colour to her perfect skin; that during such moments she possessed more than ordinary beauty.

She looked up now at the stranger, who drew in his breath sharply. His eyes widened a little, then narrowed. His grip upon her tightened, and he drew her slowly nearer. As she read his purpose she began to struggle. It was useless. She was helpless in that iron grip.

"You must not . . . shall not," she breathed. "You will not dare . . ."

Her gasping words were halted as with a deft movement he seized the hood of her cloak, forcing her head to remain still, and his lips came down on hers, softly at first, then harder. He kissed her long and lingeringly till she felt her senses swimming.

He released her so abruptly that she staggered and almost fell. His expression held anger and something which might have been disgust. He began to speak, but Georgina, blind and deaf to anything but her humiliated rage, struck him across the face with her open hand as hard as she could. Then she picked up her skirts and ran. Eliza backed away, one hand to her mouth, before she too raced away.

They did not stop until they were out of the Kennerley woods and safe on the Havard estate, but Eliza heard her mistress repeating, as she panted for breath, "How dare he? How dare he?"

When they finally paused, their quick breath clouding the freezing air, Eliza said smugly, "Tell your brother, miss. He'll call him out for his insolence."

"You will never breathe a word of what happened to anyone," flashed Georgina. "Promise me, you'll not tell."

Eliza backed away before the tempest in her mistress's eyes. "I promise, miss, 'pon my honour."

But Georgina guessed that within minutes the servants' hall would be abuzz with gossip about the insult put upon Miss Havard. She opened the gate which led into the pleasure grounds, looking sadly at the decaying weeds which would soon strangle the spring time growth of flowers, and wondered how the grass over which they sped would be scythed this year. Then she glanced upward to try to see if the chimney pots had reached a dangerous state of disrepair.

The door opened before she could ring, and the old Steward took Georgina's cloak, while Eliza slipped away eager to impart her delicious gossip.

"Thank you, Henry," murmured Georgina. She knew it was useless to protest his long wait for her in a hall whose chill was scarcely softened by the tiny fire. He had begun work as a page for her grandfather and had been pensioned off into a neat cottage five years before, but Henry had no illusions about the Havard fortunes, and he came daily to try to take the places of the missing footmen and butler. All his devotion for his dead master had been transferred to Miss Georgina, and he looked his sorrow as he stared at her now, warming her hands at the small heap of wood ash, her skirts filthy. He saw the angry scratch on her wrist. "You've been hurt. That wound should be tended."

Georgina forced a smile. "It's nothing, Henry. A . . . .a slight accident."

She knew that as soon as he went to the servants' hall he would discover what had happened, and she felt a surge of shame and anger against the stranger who had humiliated her. Forestalling Henry's further protests, she mentioned the increasing danger of the chimney pots.

He ignored her remark and gave a deep sigh. "If my late master, your grandfather, could see how matters stand with you, he would spin in his grave. If he knew what you, a high-born young lady, were doing . . ."

"What I do is my affair and not for you to comment upon."

"True enough, but when you enter cottages where there is sickness, you expose yourself and your young brothers and sisters to danger."

This was sound truth which Georgina recognised, and she said more mildly, "I do only my duty. Ladies of this house have always gone among the villagers to give help, and I take proper precautions against spreading disease."

Henry sighed again. He believed that what she did was far in excess of what common folk had any right to expect. Georgina smiled at him. "Come, Henry, you and I must not fall out, or who will be left to care for this family?"

He sniffed. "I'll make sure your bath water is prepared."

Georgina was surprised by the flicker of flames as she entered her room. Fires were a luxury that were now afforded only in her mother's bedchamber, and she felt guilty at her brief loss of patience with the old man as she realised that he must have carried up the precious coals himself.

The circular bath was set out on the fireside rug, and Eliza carried in two large cans, one of hot and one of cold water. Georgina removed all her clothes and washed herself with the care recommended by Luke Musgrove, the apothecary, who insisted that dirt and disease went hand in hand.

Eliza then helped her into a white muslin dress with the tiny sleeves and low neck favoured for her daughters by Mrs. Havard, who was much given to wondering vociferously what they should do when their clothes wore out, or worse, if the fashions should change so drastically as to render their entire wardrobes useless.

Georgina had given up pointing out that it would scarcely

matter, since they possessed only one ancient carriage drawn by the work horses when they could be spared from the home farm, and were unable to visit distant friends in the old style. Refusing to condescend to the half-world of wealthy farmers and traders, Mrs. Havard remained at home, discussing endlessly with Georgina's seventeen-year-old sister, Penelope, the life she once had led and into which she saw no chance of introducing her children.

When Georgina said that these conversations made Penelope even more discontented, and that her sister should be trying to learn some gainful occupation, Mrs. Havard simply moaned and reached for her smelling salts.

Now Georgina pulled a comb through her hair, which she dragged back into an unbecoming knot around which she tied a green ribbon. She completed her toilette with a soft, white woollen shawl knitted by herself to the disgust of her mother and Penelope, who reasoned that the making of useful garments should be left to the lower orders.

She glanced into her looking glass to confirm that she was neat, and Eliza's reflected eyes met hers and held them. In the maid's was the knowledge of Georgina's insult in the woods mixed with contempt for a family whose daughter could be mistaken for a governess. For a family whose servants were so few that their services could not be defined, so that she herself could be called upon to work in the kitchens, bed-chambers or, as now, as a makeshift dresser.

Georgina felt a little sick, but pride gave her head a lift, and she said, "You may go, Eliza."

The girl dropped a mocking curtsey and left Georgina staring at her own reflection. The fire was dying and the room growing dark in the light from a solitary candle. For an instant she seemed to see another face looking over her shoulder; a dark face with eyes of grey steel which mocked her helplessness, and she shivered as she turned away and sped downstairs.

The drawing room needed the brilliance of sunlight to

emphasise the growing shabbiness; now it looked invitingly cosy in the light of candles and the large fire which burned in any room graced by Mrs. Havard. She and Penelope were engaged in fashioning landscapes in coloured silks which, when framed, were hung in prominent places throughout the Hall. Georgina was hard put to decide which of them produced the most garish results.

Her mother looked up and asked her usual question. "You've thoroughly cleansed yourself?"

"I have, ma'am. I always do."

She walked to the fireplace, holding out her chilly hands to the glow. "I believe Mr. Musgrove has cured that poor girl I spoke of earlier. Only think of it, Mama, such a long-standing putrid disease of the leg responding to so simple a remedy as an infusion of malt and a carrot poultice. The inflammation is much reduced, and Mr. Musgrove believes that when the young carrots are in season, her cure will be complete. He says . . ."

"Must you always speak of disease and filth?" interrupted Penelope. "Mama, stop her I beg of you. My stomach will not bear such conversation."

Mrs. Havard was in a dilemma which was as familiar as it was distressing. She fully agreed with Penelope that a young lady of barely nineteen years should be unaware of such matters. Yet if she said so, they would be subjected to one of Georgina's dissertations about the right of women to become what they wished, as advocated by that dreadful Mary Wollstonecraft. Would to God they had never engaged the governess who had introduced the writings of that indecent female to her daughters. Fortunately Penelope had not been tainted, but Georgina had seized avidly at the new ideals and now worked in the parish in a way no respectable female should dream of doing.

She glanced at the clock. "Cook is late with dinner again," she quavered. "It is almost half past the hour, and she knows I hate to wait past five o'clock for my dinner in the country. Matters were better arranged in your father's day. He would not have supported such dilatory behaviour."

Georgina bit her lip to prevent the retort that if her father had not behaved so recklessly they would be able to employ the necessary domestics to ensure their comfort.

She had seldom met her father, he being too busy in the pursuit of pleasure to spare time to his children who, along with debts, were his entire legacy. She had known her mother little better, since she had previously come home only to produce another baby with the minimum of trouble and the maximum complaint, then cheerfully abandon each one to a growing army of nurses and a succession of governesses.

Sometimes Havard Hall had been all bustling activity and laughter when her parents entertained grand folk and their often grander servants, when Georgina and her brothers and sisters would be summoned to the drawing room for an hour, to be cooed over then forgotten.

So the news that their father had lost all his money in one reckless fling, then conveniently died of a purulent fever had made little impression on the young Havards. It was when their mother returned home to stay permanently, to fill their ears with bitter regrets; when clothes wore out and were patched; when servants left and were not replaced, that they realised the difference in their circumstances.

Mr. Havard had one son by his first wife; Peregrine was almost twenty-one and rioting his way through Oxford. The Hall was entailed on him, otherwise, as Mrs. Havard never wearied of explaining, they would have no home at all. "As it is," she said constantly, "we are here only on his sufferance. When he finds himself a wife . . ." The sentence was always concluded by a long sigh, and her children gathered that in the event of such a calamity they would be destitute indeed, as their Mama's jointure brought in a paltry three hundred pounds a year and she could save nothing from the estate income which dwindled yearly.

At dinner they were joined by the two elder members of the nursery, fifteen-year-old Lucilla and Edmund who, at fourteen, had grown sullen since his enforced withdrawal from Harrow. He avoided his mother's arms, thrown wide in a theatrical greeting, and parried her questions regarding the day's work. Mrs. Havard smiled archly at him. "This will not do, my son. If you do not study, how will you follow your brother to Oxford?"

With distress Georgina noted the curl of his lip, but no one pointed out to the fond mama the obvious fact that, as matters stood, the only chance Edmund would have in the world would be perhaps as a tutor in a third rate school.

Lucilla submitted to her mother's petting. "How have you fared today, my darling? Miss Pearce tells me that you take little thought for your embroidery, but spend far too much time poring over books. I cannot have my pretty little daughter ruining her eyes, you know, and besides . . ."

She allowed the sentence to peter out as her eyes strayed to Georgina, who sensed the unspoken words. Lucilla must not resemble her eldest sister, who took an unnatural interest in sick folk instead of pursuing the occupations of a lady.

After dinner Mrs. Havard made her daily visit to the nurseries to inspect the rest of her surviving brood, two charming little girls and a sturdy boy, then sat in the drawing room, watching the others play at Lottery Tickets and filling in the few quiet moments with dire predictions for the future.

Lucilla and Edmund had been sent to bed and the three ladies sat drinking their tea when Henry appeared, bearing a silver tray on which lay a note with a splendid seal.

Mrs. Havard looked puzzled. She turned it over and over in her hand. "Who can have sent it?" she wondered aloud.

"Perhaps if you opened it, Mama," gently suggested Georgina.

Mrs. Havard did so, read its brief contents, and gave a little shriek.

"Mama," cried Penelope, always ready to support her

mother in any display of emotion, "are you ill? Is it bad news? Georgina, don't stand gaping, but bring some hartshorn."

Mrs. Havard waved her daughter away, keeping a surprisingly firm hold upon the note, which Penelope endeavoured to wrest from her. "I am perfectly well, thank you. Stop your fidgets, do.

"Penelope, Georgina, what do you think? Robert Kennerley is in residence with a large party and wishes us to dine with them tomorrow."

There was a brief silence before Penelope clasped her small white hands. "Oh, Mama, at last an invitation we can accept. Oh, say we will go, do, please. Who can tell what persons we may meet there? Lord Kennerley is young —his friends . . ."

Her eyes met her mother's with perfect understanding. For the first time in her life Penelope might meet young men of fortune and address. This was the opportunity for which they had longed.

Mrs. Havard looked for an instant at Georgina and could not hide her doubts that her eldest daughter could ever appear to advantage with her thin pale face and too-slender figure.

But Penelope! Mrs. Havard's face bore a tender expression and her eyes lit with joy as she regarded Penelope. With her softly curling hair of purest gold; her large blue eyes and thick brown lashes; her delicately arched brows and perfect complexion of pink and cream; her gracefully rounded figure; she could not fail to enhance any company, be it the highest in the land.

And there might be some personable young man, wellborn, possessed of fortune, who would be enchanted sufficiently by her daughter to wish to pursue the acquaintance. And once captivated by such loveliness, how could he fail to offer marriage? Mrs. Havard's mind darted ahead. What could follow then? A town house—the Season with opportunities for the others—even Georgina?

Mrs. Havard looked once more at her eldest child and could have shaken her until her teeth rattled, she was so frustrated to see that her habitually calm demeanor was not one whit changed by the news.

She had no way of knowing the immense effort which kept Georgina's apparent serenity as she contemplated that one of the party at Kennerley would be the tall stranger whose memory filled her with angry shame.

CHAPTER 2

It took only two minutes of excited exclamation on the part of Penelope and her mother to reach the point at which they thought of clothes.

"Mama!" cried Penelope, "what will I wear?"

Mrs. Havard thought deeply. On questions of such importance she was able to bring unusual concentration of mind. Since settling in the country their few new garments had been sewn by the Misses Tomkins, genteely poor daughters of a deceased clergyman, who assured Mrs. Havard that only the deepest respect for her and her family would have allowed them to set aside their charitable work and insert their exquisite stitchery into the muslins and silks occasionally brought to them by the ladies of the Hall.

Everyone knew that they sewed far into the night by the light of too few candles, working for any farmer's wife with money to spare, but their deception was forgiven.

Mrs. Havard said, "It is fortunate, my love, that Miss Emily Tomkins has received the fashion plates from London before she commenced your new white muslin. To be sure they are a trifle out-dated, but will have to serve. The embroidery will enhance the dress and I will send a message instantly that they are to be sure to have it ready for a fitting by forenoon and finished later in the day, though they have your precise measurements and should . . ."

Here the chatter penetrated Georgina's reverie, which was concentrated on selecting and rejecting reasons for not appearing at Lord Kennerley's dinner party. It would look extremely odd should she refuse, as Robert Kennerley was a childhood friend of herself and Peregrine and, although three years her senior, had regarded her as an equal. She clearly recalled his messages of sympathy when at the age of twelve she had been discovered riding her pony astride—skirts hitched to a scandalous level which showed inches of her cotton drawers—and had been whipped and locked in her room.

He and Peregrine, on vacation from Harrow, had thought it a great lark when she lowered a basket from the window to receive tidbits filched from the Havard and Kennerley kitchens to augment her punitive diet.

"How far has the embroidery advanced?" she asked.

Mrs. Havard and Penelope stared at her. "I cannot be sure," answered her mother.

"Oh, Mama," exclaimed Penelope, "we gave them no cause to suppose we should require the dress so soon. What if they have put it aside . . ."

"Nonsense, my love." Mrs. Havard frowned. "They will, of course, finish work for us before any other consideration."

"Which Miss Tomkins has engaged to embroider the dress?" asked Georgina.

"You are very full of questions, miss," said her mother sharply. "Of what possible consequence can it be to you . . . ?"

"I think it is Miss Lucy," interrupted Penelope. "Or was it Miss Emily? They look so alike—both old and withered."

"I ask because Miss Lucy has been advised by Mr. Musgrove to work only in daylight. Her eyes are too often inflamed by sewing far into the night."

Mrs. Havard went pink with indignation. "I'm sure it is no fault of mine if her eyes are so poor, for all the work *I* am able to give her . . ."

"I must have the dress, Georgina," wailed Penelope. "You would not know, but the fashion plates show a greater quantity of embroidery around the hem at present. I cannot be disgraced before the other ladies. You would not have me appear in last year's fashions!"

"No indeed," agreed Mrs. Havard, "Georgina had no such thought. Well, I will send candles with my message so that there may be sufficient light, though with candles the price they are . . ."

"Could not my sister work upon her dress herself?" Georgina looked around at the silk pictures which were in varying degrees of progression.

"Make our clothes?" Mrs. Havard's plump cheeks quivered, and Penelope's beautiful lips parted.

"Many ladies do, I believe."

"Not Havard ladies," said her mother. "Ring the bell, Penelope, my love. We will send to the Misses Tomkins directly."

On the following day the weather was even colder and Mrs. Havard grumbled bitterly as she allowed Henry to help her into a heavy, fur-lined wool cloak. She then sank into a chair and permitted him to kneel and place pattens on her feet. He performed the same service for Penelope, and Georgina arrived in the hall in time to see him struggling to rise. She felt angry. Surely her mother could have performed this small duty herself, or at least sent for a maid. She used Henry as if he were properly employed and made no allowance for his age and rheumatism. She would speak to Mr. Musgrove about a different remedy. She dared not address Henry on the subject as he would be embarrassed by any mention of bodily infirmity by one of the young ladies.

Penelope drew the hood of her scarlet cloak about her face

and Georgina marvelled again at her beauty. She had little in common with her sister, but she cared enough for her to hope she would be happily settled in life. For Penelope this meant acquiring money, which seemed impossible. Mrs. Havard also looked at her younger daughter and her expression softened. The thought of such a beauty mouldering unseen in the depths of the country was more than she could bear. Her eyes slid to Georgina and she wondered yet once more how an accredited beauty such as she had been and handsome Havard had produced such a changeling.

Georgina had slept badly, her dreams troubled by grey eyes which tormented and mocked her. Her thin face was almost colourless and her hair lacklustre. It almost tempted one, thought her mother, to look upon the only male with whom she seemed on happy terms in a favourable light—until one remembered that he was only an apothecary and as such little better than a servant.

She slid her hands into the warm muff which Henry held for her and said, "Come, Penelope, if we walk briskly we should not suffer too greatly from the cold. At least the worst of the mud will be frozen solid—in which case we might not need our pattens. I wonder, should we wear them . . . oh, that I should be brought to such a dilemma. In your father's day we had carriages and horses for all occasions, did we not, Henry?"

"Indeed yes, ma'am. Can I be of service to you? This morning on my way here my feet almost froze to the ground."

Mrs. Havard sighed. "No, I thank you. Miss Penelope and I have agreed already that we must make the journey ourselves so that the sewing will not be stopped for an instant."

When the two ladies returned, their discomfort from the cold was quite forgotten in the joy that the gown was a perfect fit, the embroidery was exquisite, and all would be made ready in good time.

Georgina slipped out soon afterward to visit the two elderly ladies herself and to take a bottle of Hungary water to use on the smarting eyes. Miss Lucy thanked her, but remained close to the window, her needle darting swiftly in and out of the white muslin.

Miss Emily fluttered around, insisting that Georgina partake of violet cakes and sycamore wine . . . "of which," she assured Georgina, "your dear Grandmama was so fond. Many times during the course of her parish visits she was gracious enough to compliment us when she called here.

"How well I remember seeing her upright figure seated in her carriage as the footman went into some cottage or other to bestow food or medicine . . ." She stopped, flushing, feeling that Miss Havard might think she was being critical. But Georgina said levelly, "I prefer to supervise matters myself, Miss Emily. Please, Miss Lucy, do not neglect your eyes."

"Indeed she will not." Miss Emily was glad to change the subject and assured her dear Miss Havard that her sister always wore a Burgundy-pitch plaster between her shoulders and regularly bathed her feet in warm water.

During the day Mrs. Havard had enjoyed a talk with Webster, her personal maid of many years, who, though deeming below-stairs gossip to be beneath her, kept her ears sharp enough to keep her mistress informed of any useful snippets. Mrs. Havard was therefore able to impart to her daughters the gratifying information that several young men of consequence were gathered at Kennerley.

"There are ladies too, but I fancy that my Penelope will not find one to hold a candle to her for looks. The Earl of Rivington is present, but you girls need not consider him."

Penelope's blue eyes opened wide. "Why, Mama, is he so dreadful?"

"Not at all. He is eight and twenty, a handsome man and very rich, but he will never deign to notice you. He has travelled in all parts of the world not spoilt by Bonaparte; he has partaken of every kind of sport and pleasure to be had by a man of means and fashion. Even before I retired from society he had become bored beyond anything by his activities, and above all by the young women who tried to attract him.

"I believe he will end by marrying Charlotte Ingram. He must have an heir, and it is certain that she had been dangling after him since her come-out three years since. She has spurned many an aspiring suitor, but she will be so wealthy she may please herself."

"If he is so tired of pleasure, I wonder he does not enlist," said Georgina. "I am sure our country needs men to fight."

"A lot you know, miss," snapped Mrs. Havard. "He is his Mama's only surviving child, and she dotes on him. They say it would kill her to lose him."

That evening Webster helped Mrs. Havard into a dress of lavender silk embroidered with silver and pinned at the shoulder by her best remaining piece of jewellery, a large amethyst brooch set in diamonds. Neither woman mentioned the fact that the gown was out of date. All the money that could be spared was used to procure clothes for Penelope, Mrs. Havard believing that Georgina did not care for clothes. She was not entirely correct in her assumption. Her eldest daughter did not make clothes her main interest, but she took great delight in textures and colours.

She stood now clad in her chemise, her arms goosefleshed with cold as Eliza helped her into a round dress of pale green muslin. The colour suited her, giving her skin a slightly translucent quality and emphasizing the green in her eyes. Her mother, with a belated memory of what was due to the eldest daughter, having given Penelope first choice, sent Webster with her jewel box, from which Georgina selected a filigree gold chain with tiny pearls and matching earrings and bracelets. She completed her outfit with a silk printed shawl of white and green and felt she looked well.

Yet Penelope so outshone her in her white and gold loveliness that Georgina's small glow of satisfaction faded when she saw her. Over Penelope's shoulders lay a gauzy white scarf, and the only colour came from her deep blue eyes, her shining gold hair and the tiny pinpoint flashes of her mother's modest diamond necklace and eardrops.

Not all the stable lad's currying and combing had disguised the fact that the horses were thick-set work animals, and Mrs. Havard averted her eyes as she stepped into the old coach, feeling thankful that darkness would hide their arrival at Kennerley.

Creevy, the elderly coachman, obliged like the others to vary his duties, had on this unexpected summons joyfully refurbished his plush breeches and cocked hat and polished his brass buttons. His grandson, a tall youth of seventeen had been fitted into an unused footman's livery and now sprang clumsily to the back of the coach. The driver cracked his whip, the horses moved ponderously forward, and the Havard ladies were drawn down the long unkempt drive.

Kennerley was ablaze with lighted candles and Mrs. Havard drew a breath of pleasure at this return to former joys. She was received by a happy Robert Kennerley, who associated her with boyhood days, and who beamed at the sight of his former playmate. "It is good to see you, George. You're a breath of spring after the London beauties."

Georgina was divided by discomfiture at the doubtful compliment and nostalgia at hearing her old nickname; then her impish humour came to the fore, and she responded warmly.

"Equally pleasing to see you, my lord. I had no idea that Kennerley could appear to such advantage."

Robert grinned. "The old gentleman is probably spinning in his grave, but bless his farthing-pinching ways, for they have left me extremely forward with the world."

Georgina looked quizzically at him. He and her brother had spent some time together at Oxford and she suspected that little learning had penetrated either skull which did not relate to bloodstock, gaming, and wine. He caught her look and translated it correctly.

"Do not vex yourself, George. Now I have left Oxford I

intend to become a model squire, as many tenants will soon learn, to their advantage."

Georgina's warm response was unnoticed by Robert, who was staring past her. She looked round to see Penelope, who had paused briefly to look at her appearance in a downstairs mirror just before entering the room.

"That . . . that cannot be your sister!"

"Why not?" asked Georgina.

"Because she's only in the schoolroom—a plump little female with yaller hair."

"Time can make a difference in a girl."

But the Viscount wasn't listening. He was bowing low over her sister's hand and murmuring words which made her simper with delight.

Mrs. Havard settled herself in a corner among the dowagers and chaperons, who were twittering like starlings as they brought her up to date with the town gossip.

Groups of elegantly dressed men and women were standing or sitting about the room and, knowing no one, Georgina seated herself on a bench against the wall to enjoy the brilliant scene. A trill of laughter came from a party a few feet away, and Georgina turned to see a smiling young woman showing perfect white teeth in a face of exquisite beauty. Her silky dark hair, dressed by an expert, was entwined with diamonds and pearls which matched her costly necklace and eardrops. Her deceptively simple white gown was designed to enhance her well-proportioned figure, and her eyes were dark and glowing.

Georgina caught her breath. Was she an example of the London beauties? She looked over at Penelope and was relieved to see her well attended by gentlemen, although it was clear by now that the gowns made by the Misses Tomkins were out of date in style. She felt a flash of annoyance and was instantly ashamed that she should be troubled by so inconsequential a matter. She told herself that tomorrow she would be much happier explaining to Mr. Musgrove that

Lord Kennerley was not indifferent to the plight of his tenants.

At that moment, Lord Kennerley's hostess, his Aunt Sophia Hawke, still dazzled by her good fortune at being rescued from a life of straitened circumstances to care for his needs, realised with dismay that Miss Havard had been sitting for some time alone and unintroduced to anybody.

In her haste to remedy her oversight she hustled Georgina from one group to another in a welter of presentations and apologies until they arrived at the one containing the beautiful young woman. Georgina realised that it had been joined by another man. Even from behind she recognised the tall, powerful frame in the long-tailed coat of blue-black cloth, his muscular legs in cream breeches and silk stockings. He waited politely as Georgina met the ladies.

"Miss Charlotte Ingram," fluttered Miss Hawke, and Georgina received a cool stare from the dark-haired beauty, whose eyes clearly proclaimed that she did not see Miss Havard as a rival in any way, she being plain to a degree and wearing country-cut clothes and paltry jewels. She gave a frosty bow and turned back to her companions.

As Miss Hawke reached the man, Georgina felt an agony of apprehension which seemed to drain the blood from her legs. She caught only three words from the presentation. "Lord Alexander Rivington."

This then was the man of whom her Mama had warned them. Her adversary of the woods who was so wearied by life that he must insult unprotected women for his amusement. Georgina looked as boldly as she dared into the stony grey eyes and tried not to think of the passion they could contain. She waited in terror for his words.

"Charmed," murmured his lordship insincerely as he gave her a bow which was little lower than Miss Ingram's. Georgina realised with a shock that he did not recognise her.

Her relief lasted till, a few moments later, she was seated for dinner between two gentlemen who applied themselves either to eating or flirting with ladies known to them. Then slowly, insidiously she began to feel resentful. She told herself that he could not be expected to associate the bedraggled "governess" he had first rescued, then insulted, with Miss Havard in all the finery she could muster. She accepted that she had no claim to beauty, but to be so forgettable that a man could kiss her one day and ignore her the next was exceedingly harrowing.

She despised herself for her weakness; she recited passages to herself from Miss Wollstonecraft's book on women's rightful place in society. It was to no avail. She felt miserable and rejected and knew that, on this first real test, she was reacting like a typical female with the vapours. Sitting silently at the dinner table, among some of Polite Society's most glittering adornments, Georgina felt her world turning upside down as her values seemed to be disintegrating in the cold light of a pair of bored, grey eyes.

CHAPTER 3

Course succeeded delicious course, but Georgina's agitation, coupled with a sparing appetite, almost destroyed her wish to eat. She noticed that her mama was indulging in her love of rich foods on this rare opportunity and that Penelope also was eating as if tomorrow would bring no victuals. Their mother had often said with meaningful looks at Georgina's slender frame that gentlemen liked a female who was well rounded, but Georgina guessed that one day Penelope would become as plump as Mama—and she had better be wed before that happened.

A beauty without a fortune might be lucky enough to attract a rich husband; a fat girl in such circumstances would fail completely.

Once only dared she look down the long silver-adorned table at Lord Rivington. She stared at his saturnine face for a moment then, as if he sensed her scrutiny, he turned his head quickly and for an instant seemed to catch the hostility in her eyes. Puzzlement wrinkled his brow; they held glances for a shade too long for polite acquaintances before Georgina's eyelids hid her too-expressive eyes.

She must be more careful. She had only to endure this evening without his remembering her and she would be safe from embarrassment. It was unlikely they would again move in the same circles.

Back in the drawing room after dinner, Mrs. Havard gossiped happily and made mental notes of the changed fashions so that she could bring the Misses Tomkins up to date, while she watched with approval as Penelope held the attention of several beaux. Georgina sat alone again, ignored by everyone save the kind Miss Hawke. Surely she could make some effort to please, sighed her mother inwardly, but maybe it was as well she should remain inconspicuous. Unblessed as she seemed to be by looks or accomplishment, she could succeed only in drawing adverse comment to herself if she behaved like a beauty.

Mrs. Havard could not know that her daughter was praying quietly for the evening to end before the Earl of Rivington's memory was restored. As it was, Georgina had caught several questioning glances directed her way and felt sure he was aware that he should know her.

She listened to snippets of conversation until abruptly her attention was riveted by the name "Wollstonecraft."

"I collect," said a red-haired girl, "that she advocates that any young woman who so desires should receive as liberal an education as her brothers and become a member of a profession."

"My dearest," shrilled a matron, "from where did you obtain such knowledge? From no book in our home, that I vow. And if your school allowed such reading, I will make my protest when I return to London."

"Lord, Mama, you make such a bother. I have never read anything of that nature." She spoke confidingly to her companions in a voice clearly intended for the whole room. "I am not allowed even to attend the Circulating Library to obtain novels, though many of my friends do so. They are not so harshly treated."

The lively discussion which broke out among the dowagers regarding the merits or otherwise of novel-reading was interrupted by a gentle voice. It seemed that Miss Ingram's wealth and beauty commanded instant attention. "I read a novel sometimes," she said, "but mama trusts me to know when I should put the book aside, should I reach a passage unsuitable for a young woman."

A murmur of approval rippled through the company, and a young man in a blue satin waistcoat applauded gently, "I have said these many times that ladies, and indeed gentlemen only of a high standing should be encouraged to read. Education of the lower orders gives them a quite ridiculous belief in their importance. One begins to find astonishing manners in quite common people nowadays."

Miss Ingram continued as if he had not spoken. "I use Mrs. Hannah More as my standard. She once stated that our sex is too unstable and capricious to be capable of governing any save those in our domestic circle, and that even there no creature is so much indebted to its subordination for its good behaviour as a woman."

"Flummery!" The word rang loud and clear as Georgina sprang to her feet, this last speech proving too much for her self control.

Everyone in the large, brilliantly lighted room stared at her. Eyebrows were raised; fans stopped fluttering, quizzing glasses were levelled in her direction. In her indignation she saw none of it.

"Women should be educated and I mean women of all classes. They should be allowed to live as they wish, to become attorneys, members of Parliament, anything they choose.

"And if they do not feel equal to public life, then let them use their education for raising their children to a higher degree of learning. Ignorant mothers make bad mothers, who are likely to rear poor, weak children.

"I am the believer not the originator of these sentiments. They are Miss Wollstonecraft's, whom you revile without having read her writings. I tell you if its precepts were followed and women held control, the world would be a fairer place; perhaps there would even be an end to war."

There was complete silence as she finished. Even the footmen had stopped moving. Then the quiet was broken by a sound Georgina recognised. It was that of her mother gasping in the first throes of a spasm.

She was assiduously attended by her friends and Georgina sat down, feeling as if her legs would fail her. What had possessed her? She felt an unprecedented desire to join her mother by having a fit of hysterics, bit her lips hard to prevent their shaking, and feeling as vulnerable as a naughty child, she clenched her hands tightly beneath the folds of her shawl.

A cool voice cut across the angry murmur which had begun. A voice ringing with authority which demands and expects attention. It even had the effect of bringing Mrs. Havard out of her spasm.

Lord Rivington, leaning nonchalantly against a wall, his arms loosely folded said, "I have read Miss Wollstonecraft's book. It is not one which has much literary merit, and I am amazed that it could fill any young woman with such a rebellious spirit as seems to possess Miss Havard. Yet I did hear of a family of four young females who read her and became quite emancipated.

"Between them they groomed horses, set up a literary salon, experimented on their pets, and actually boasted of their muscles. None of these accomplishments seems to me desirable in a young lady, though I daresay they were exaggerated, as is the way of the world."

His speech produced a shout of laughter from the men and

even the ladies, amid protestations, joined in the merriment.

Georgina sat quite still, her eyes downcast, hating Lord Rivington for his mockery. She became aware that someone was standing before her and raised her head to look straight into the face of the Earl, who was now grimly serious. For a moment hazel eyes bright with unshed tears of humiliation met grey, and she realised with a shock that her outburst had led to recognition.

She was not aware that her passionate defence of her beliefs had brought colour flaring into her pale cheeks and the brilliance of flashing emeralds to her eyes.

Lord Rivington held out a slender white hand. "Please, Miss Havard, would you favour me with a turn about the room?"

Feeling that anything would be better than sitting alone to be mocked any longer, she rose and placing icy fingertips upon the Earl's arm began to pace the floor.

For a few turns they walked in silence, their progress watched by several mamas whose hopes for their daughters were secretly fixed on this highly desirable man. Georgina kept her eyes firmly ahead, but she was perfectly conscious that many people must be following her every movement.

Lord Rivington spoke so suddenly that she started. "Yesterday in the woods I was grossly at fault. I can only beg your pardon."

"I see," she replied coldly, supposing that his noble lordship believed that an apology would make complete amends.

He continued to speak above her unresponsive head. "One could scarcely have expected to discover a respectable young woman wandering in the woods clad as you were and with only a maid-servant for protection."

"Is it then your practice to take advantage of women when you discover them to be vulnerable and of a lower order than your own?"

She felt the arm beneath her fingers grow taut as he grated, "No, it is not, madam. Is it your practice to wander abroad, inviting insults first by dressing like a scrub-woman, then behaving with provocation to unknown men?"

Georgina gasped. "Provocation! I merely fondled your dog, sir, and I had no cause to fear I might meet a . . . a libertine."

"I am no libertine, madam," he hissed.

"Then I can only felicitate you upon your portrayal to me. It was masterly. Perhaps, my lord, if you had not been so high-born, you could have made your fortune as a theatre player."

The Earl halted in mid-step, and Georgina said sweetly, "Pray do not stop walking, sir, we have attracted attention enough."

His arm was so rigid now she guessed that he would have liked to shake her, and she raised her head to look full into his face, her eyes glowing with defiant anger.

The Earl swore softly. "Miss Havard, once more you deliberately provoke me, yet perhaps you would find it in yourself to forgive me if I confess the truth."

"Which is?"

"That yesterday I was so overcome by your beauty and charms that I did not stop to think. I only felt. I wanted to kiss you and I did. I am sorry to have offended you."

Georgina gasped. Her step quickened as she raged, "Such a confession would, I collect, overcome the objections of some females. Foolish women who have been induced by men to believe that they are the weaker sex and that the attraction of their physical attributes excuses all.

"So now, not content with attacking my person, you make fun of my appearance. Return me to my mother's side. At once!" she demanded as she saw him open his mouth for what she knew would be further insincere protestations.

Lord Rivington obeyed and bade her a brief farewell through clenched teeth. Mrs. Havard, whose hopes had been raised that somehow her willful daughter had attracted the Earl, saw his face dark with anger and allowed her welcom-

ing smile to fade. Georgina rewarded his stiff bow with the
smallest possible curtsey and a look of contempt. He hurried
to the other side of the room, where he stood glowering and
drinking a glass of wine.

Georgina sank to the bench near her mother, feeling like a
child who would like to creep for protection beneath her
mother's skirts and recalling her last speech to the Earl with
shame. Would he wonder if her fury had exploded because
he had insulted her intellect or because she cared enough for
his opinion to resent his ridicule of her obvious lack of
beauty? What a fool she had been! Her sister, or Miss Ingram, would have accepted his compliments with a laugh.
Only they, she concluded miserably, would never find themselves in so degrading a position.

Georgina glanced at her mother and received the full basi-
lisk glare directed her way, as Mrs. Havard contemplated
this most embarrassing member of her family. She knew she
would get the lash of her mother's tongue later.

A soft voice cut through her gloom. "How well you spoke,
Miss Havard. I so admire a woman of courage."

She turned eagerly, feeling a flare of delight that another
should share her views, to be disappointed by the sight of
Miss Ingram, who joined her on the bench. Although the
sweetly moulded lips were curved in a smile, the eyes were
hostile.

"So brave of you," she continued, "to show a spirit of
rebellion. Alas, we poor females—why, I myself was once
soundly whipped by my governess for expressing a liberal
viewpoint. Then she, good creature, introduced me to the
works of Mrs. Hannah More and I knew her to be right. I
collect that you have read her words."

"Yes," agreed Georgina, "and I find them utterly nau-
seating. Why should we be considered inferior? Why should
we be treated only as a man's plaything, fit simply to obey
and adore him . . . ?"

She stopped, flushing crimson, as she realised that once

more she had attracted adverse attention to herself. She saw a flash of triumph in Miss Ingram's dark eyes and followed her gaze to where Lord Rivington had paused a few feet from them.

Had he been about to approach her again? She remembered her mother saying that Miss Ingram had waited for years to capture the Earl. Had she been deliberately provoked to another unseemly display? Lord Rivington walked towards them. He gave Georgina one unfathomable glance before holding out his arm to the willing lady beside her, and she was left sitting alone. The looks now being sent by Mrs. Havard scorched into her brain, and for the rest of the evening she remained among the dowagers, who ignored her.

Waiting only until the carriage door was closed, Mrs. Havard began her tirade. "Never have I been so mortified! I knew you must be without shame to conduct yourself as you do daily—without a grain of delicacy—yet I had thought you were sufficiently imbued with the principles of a gentlewoman to be taken safely into society. Could you not have held your tongue if only for your sister's sake?"

Georgina longed to defend herself, but could find no words. She suddenly felt intolerably weary and sat subdued and unhappy as the ancient carriage lumbered creakily along the rutted roads and her mother's berating voice kept pace with the wheels.

It was with profound relief that she escaped to the seclusion of her bedchamber, but the oblivion of sleep evaded her. She lay staring into the darkness, reliving the past scenes and wishing she had acted with discretion. When she drifted into slumber her dreams held mocking laughter, derisive voices and scornful eyes. One pair, grey and cold, grew larger in her fevered mind, expanding till they filled her world, compelling her to submit to imprisoning arms till she awoke, fighting the bed sheets which her tossing had tightened round her, moaning and struggling.

"I hate him! I hate him!" she cried to the empty darkness.

Her overburdened emotions found relief in tears and toward dawn she slept, waking at ten o'clock, heavy-eyed and unrefreshed.

She sat sipping her hot chocolate and reviewed all that had recently happened. "Georgina Havard," she told herself severely, "you are a fool." What cared she that she did not fit into a shallow, worthless society? She had work to do. And today she would go to visit a village woman whose latest child was tightly bound, in spite of clear evidence that such treatment in the cases of her many previous children twisted, rather than straightened, their limbs.

Dressing herself in the brown dress and taking her cloak from a closet, she went downstairs, feeling secure in the knowledge that her mother never rose before eleven. This morning she was wrong. Mrs. Havard, in lace cap and voluminous morning gown, awaited her in the breakfast parlour.

"So, miss, I was right. You paid no heed whatsoever to my words last night. I have lain awake for hours wondering what will become of us. You well know how hard it is for me to keep up appearances, yet you destroy all my efforts by your ill-governed tongue and behaviour."

She put a hand to her head. "I should have rested this morning. I vow I am not well. What have I done to deserve such a plague of a daughter?"

Georgina spread a slice of toast with preserves and poured herself a cup of coffee.

"I do not wonder that you remain silent, miss. And here you are, in that hideous garb, about to disgrace us all again."

Georgina was surprised. "How so, ma'am?"

"Have you taken a single thought as to what the visitors to Kennerley would think should they learn of your behaviour in the village? Suppose you met a member of the house party? Have you considered that?"

Georgina flushed and spilt some coffee, and her mother clasped her hands. "So you do have some tender feelings of shame. At least I can be thankful for that. Now you will oblige me by changing out of that ridiculous gown."

"Yes, Mama. If it pleases you, then I will wait until the Kennerley party has left the neighbourhood before resuming my work."

She looked at her mother, who was angrily pushing cold meats about her plate. "Will it help, Mama, to learn that I truly regret my actions of last night? I spoke the truth, but I wish I had not embarrassed you and my sister."

Mrs. Havard was silenced for a moment. "Well," she conceded, "maybe it was not as bad as I feared. Lord Rivington seemed to single you out for attention."

"I believe he meant only to taunt me further," cried Georgina. "I detest the man!"

"Detest! You cannot detest a man whom you have met but once, especially one who so gallantly came to our rescue last night by making the company laugh."

Georgina faltered. "No . . . no, of course. It was only that he seems so proud . . . so aloof . . ."

"And with every right. He is one of the richest men in England, and his ancestry is impeccable. There is no great house closed to him."

The door opened to admit Penelope. "My love," exclaimed Mrs. Havard, "I was sure you would not yet be awake. Georgina, ring for fresh coffee. Could you not sleep, dearest?"

"Sleep! How could I after last night? Mama, I hope you have spoken to my sister."

She caught sight of Georgina's gown and gave a shriek. "Mama! You will not permit her to appear in public looking like that while the gentlemen are at Kennerley. I shall die of shame—I know I shall."

"Georgina will be changing, I can assure you. Now pray do try to eat and drink a little. You must keep up your strength."

After Penelope had made a surprisingly good meal, Mrs.

Havard rose and led the way into the morning room. It lay at the back of the house and caught the rays of the frosty sun which exposed the fading of the draperies. A bright fire burned, and Mrs. Havard sat close and pulled her embroidery frame toward her. Penelope reclined on a sofa on the other side of the fireplace and gazed into the flames, a little smile curving her lips. She looked exquisite in her softly flowing gown of pale blue, her shoulders veiled in a black lace shawl.

Georgina, who had followed them to fetch a book to take to her room, felt a sudden pang of remorse. Had she really spoiled her sister's chances?

Mrs. Havard looked up. "Georgina, do not I beg, stand there gaping in that foolish manner. Please be so good as to obey me by changing your dress."

"Very well, Mama, and if you will excuse me I believe I will remain in my room. There is something I wish to study."

"Some book lent you by that apothecary, no doubt, and quite unsuited to a young woman."

"It is merely *Domestic Medicine* by Mr. Buchan and intended for family reading. I find it fascinating. Do you know . . . ?"

Penelope held up a languid hand and shuddered. "Please spare us your hideous details of disease. Mama, make her stop. After so restless a night I could not bear to listen."

"Your sister is right. Go to your room and if you must act like a . . . like a . . . *man,* do not expect us to participate in your astonishing interests."

Georgina turned to leave and was confronted by Henry, who in tones of deep satisfaction, announced: "You have guests, madam. Miss Charlotte Ingram; Lord Alexander Rivington; Lord Robert Kennerley; Sir Stannard Morton."

Three pairs of incredulous eyes met his before he stood aside to allow the visitors to enter the room.

CHAPTER

Miss Ingram tripped lightly across the faded carpet and held out a hand. "Dear Mrs. Havard, pray do forgive this early call, but when I heard that Lord Kennerley was to visit his old friends, nothing would suit me but that I should accompany him. I so desired to meet you all again."

Her eyes searched the room, alighting first on the enchanting vision on the sofa and lingering on Georgina, who greeted her with assumed calm. She thought she detected a look of amused contempt as Miss Ingram exclaimed, "Dear Miss Havard, such a gay time we had last night, did we not?"

Georgina answered with a confused murmur. She had seen Lord Rivington's glance travel swiftly over her unbecoming gown. The memory of what had happened the last time he had seen her wear it made her bite her lip, but she made her curtseys before sitting quietly on the window seat.

The Earl bowed over her mother's hand. "I, too, feel the need to apologise, ma'am, but Robert argued so compellingly that it would not do to stand on ceremony with such familiar friends I was persuaded . . ."

His speech was cut short by Mrs. Havard's assurances that his visit could only do them honour, and Georgina clenched her teeth. Her mother need not humble herself; his high-flown lordship would never consider Penelope as a bride.

Her eyes strayed to the third gentleman, whom she recalled as being one of her sister's admirers of last night. Sir Stannard Morton's yellow stockinet breeches were so tight about his plump person she marvelled at his ability to sit. Gold satin waistcoat gleamed beneath a blue velvet coat, and in his enormous cravat flashed a diamond of great size and splendour.

Beyond a muttered, " 'Sarvant, ma'am," to Mrs. Havard he had not uttered a word, but sat staring at Penelope in a way which Georgina would have found disconcerting, but which that young lady appeared to accept as her due.

Once more Miss Ingram singled out Georgina, and sitting by her, gave her a dazzling smile. One delicately gloved hand smoothed her burgundy velvet pelisse, then gently touched her matching bonnet with its tall white coque feather. "Were you about to ride, Miss Havard? It is so very cold. Dear Lord Kennerley offered to mount me, but I prefer to use a carriage in such inclement weather."

"I . . . I ride very little," stammered Georgina, who felt sure that her companion must know to a penny how matters stood with them. "Why did you suppose . . . ?"

Miss Ingram gave a silvery laugh. "I do beg your pardon." Then she continued in tones which carried through the room. "I had assumed by your gown that you had stolen a march on the rest of us and were wearing some new French fashion in riding dress. I declare it is too bad of Bonaparte to deprive us of the latest Paris modes, but I am aware that some fashion plates still do reach us." She peered closely at the coarse brown stuff. "Such a—serviceable material."

Mrs. Havard's laugh was like the tinkle of ice. "Pray, Miss Ingram, allow me to offer you refreshment. You must know that my daughter does a deal of work among the poor of the parish—my own constitution does not allow me. Her gown is not one of beauty, I grant, but some of the dwellings ladies of quality are forced to visit in the pursuit of charity . . ." She sighed expressively. "Miss Ingram is right, my love, do go now and change into one of your prettiest morning gowns. The company will excuse you, I am sure."

"No, do not deprive us," begged Miss Ingram, putting out a detaining hand. "I long to know of Miss Havard's work. I am woefully ignorant, as my papa does not allow me to enter any but the homes of our well-to-do tenant farmers, and I have a great curiosity about the lives of the others."

Penelope intervened quickly, in a voice shrill with false nonchalance. "My sister undertakes all manner of tasks in an effort to conquer boredom. I declare we are hard put to find ways to amuse ourselves between engagements, and she has so much energy." She fanned herself languidly. "It makes one weary to be near her."

Georgina flushed. "I beg your pardon, Penelope, but I am never bored." Her voice, vibrant with earnestness drew all eyes to her, and the sight of Lord Rivington staring with raised brows added to her indignation. "I work among the poor because I want to. Mr. Musgrove has taught me . . ." She stopped abruptly, remembering her mother's strictures, but Miss Ingram prompted her.

"You were saying? Mr. Musgrove . . . ?" She turned to Robert Kennerley. "Was he of our company last night? I do not recall the name. No, that cannot be. Mr. Musgrove taught you, you say, then he must be your tutor. But you are not still in the schoolroom."

Deploring her wretched tongue, Georgina muttered, "He is the local apothecary."

"Apothecary? And he teaches you? Why this is quite delightful! Pray what does he teach you? Do not, I implore you, leave me in suspense."

For once Georgina wished her mother or sister would chatter of something inconsequential, but they seemed shocked into silence. "He . . . he shows me how to help the sick . . . what to do when some poor creature is in pain. I . . . I find much satisfaction . . ."

Robert joined in, "George was always a prime fixer of fallen birds and wounded animals. Nothing was too bad for her to tackle. I own I could not stomach some of the things she did. Kept a regular infirmary of creatures . . ."

He faltered as he encountered the full glare of Mrs. Havard's gaze. "Yes, well, she don't wander round collecting sick animals now, I fancy. Very good of her to trouble so much about the cottagers."

"Then last night you were serious," exclaimed Miss Ingram. "You truly believe that we females should follow a profession, should we so desire?"

Georgina was eager to make someone understand. "Oh, I was. When I read Miss Wollstonecraft's book I felt I had realised a great truth. If only I could become a physician, or even a humble apothecary, I believe . . ."

Mrs. Havard said loudly, "My daughter is merely expressing a childish dream. Why, when I think of some of the secret wishes of my girlish heart, I vow I shudder." She simpered, "She does not, of course, speak of girls of quality."

"Mama, please," begged Georgina.

Lord Rivington broke his watchful silence. "*I* believe that Miss Havard speaks sincerely. She truly desires to act the part of physician."

Georgina's eyes flashed dangerously. "I act no part, sir! I do what I think is right. If I see sights which make me shudder; if I experience offensive odours, should I turn away? If some wretched creature begs my help, must I refuse? I tell you, sir, I sometimes return home feeling sick with what I have had to perform, yet I know . . ."

She looked full into the grey eyes and encountered such amused enjoyment as caused her to stop with a gasp. Like Miss Ingram, he had been provoking her, but he had the wit to choose exactly the right words to cause her to forget herself sufficiently to use terms quite unfitted for polite company. He was fully revenged for her taunt of last night.

"My Mama suggested I should change my dress," she said, holding back a sob of anger and humiliation. "Pray excuse me." And she hurried from the room.

She had scarcely completed the change before her mother burst unceremoniously into her room and sank into a chair. Her hands were clasped over her heart, and she panted for breath.

"Mama," cried Georgina, "are you unwell?"

"Well might you ask, miss. How any daughter of mine could behave with such a lack of propriety . . . though I apprehend I must expect such conduct of *you*. And before Miss Ingram, of all people. And the gentlemen! What must they think? God only knows what stories will be circulating when they return to town, which they spoke of doing tomorrow. I shall never hold up my head again."

Although Georgina knew that they were unlikely to enter society, she felt genuine contrition. "I owe you an apology, Mama, I should not have spoken with such vehemence."

"You owe your sister a greater one," said Mrs. Havard.

"Penelope?"

"Of course, Penelope. I would have you know that Sir Stannard Morton, though only a baronet, is of unexceptionable birth and has an income of thirty thousand a year. He has an obvious tendre for your sister, but he is a great gossip and always ready to be swayed by one or another. Now he will be thinking, I have no doubt, that to consider an alliance with a family containing such a hoyden lacking all womanly grace and shame would be beneath him."

"Mama, Sir Stannard cannot have spoken to you in so short a time."

"No he has not, stupid girl. Such matters are extremely delicate, but he does not make a secret of his admiration for Penelope."

"But he must be all of forty years. Surely you would not wish Penelope to . . ."

The flood of her mother's wrath burst over her. She was left in no doubt that a gentleman of birth who could ensure a girl's entry into the highest circles, and whose income enable her to shine therein, was *never* too old to pay his addresses and that she, Georgina, had not only ruined Penelope, but her other sisters and brothers besides.

Georgina said miserably, "Surely, Mama, our little affairs can be of no consequence to them. They will forget."

"Miss Ingram will not and she will be sure to remind others. It is but two years since I retired here and I remember that one from our come-out. She is wealthy as well as beautiful and refused many brilliant offers, even in her first season, because she has set her inclination upon Lord Rivington. Now she is almost one and twenty and must marry if the world is not to whisper that she has been left upon the shelf. You have drawn the Earl's attention to you, and she will not forgive you."

"Mama, he despises me. He mocked me."

"Last night he singled you out—that is all Miss Ingram will see."

Remembering her encounters with Lord Rivington, Georgina remained silent and confused, wishing she could confide in her mother. Mrs. Havard rose, the damp chill of the room having penetrated her as the fires of her anger died. "It seems you think you know better than I. I shall leave you to reflect upon what you have done to us."

She would have been dismayed by Georgina's reflections. Georgina was wondering if it would be best for her family if she encouraged Mr. Musgrove's attention. Eventual marriage to him would mean the severance of her family ties, but she could live quietly doing the work she felt fitted for, and they would not fear she would shame them again.

She thought of Luke Musgrove's sturdy frame and honest brown eyes that burned with dedication to relieving the suffering of the poor. She tried to examine her feelings for him. Then his image was blotted out of her brain with the suddenness of a thunder clap by another. A tall, strong figure, a dark saturnine face, and a pair of taunting grey eyes, made her give a dry, shuddering sob. She could imagine with what corrosive wit the news of a marriage between herself and an apothecary would be received. It would make a good story to tell and would go well with Miss Ingram's account of the queer Miss Havard.

Well, what cared she for the opinions of London? Her future lay with folk who needed her and perhaps with an honourable man.

As she reached the downstairs hall she was surprised by the sound of carriage wheels, followed by an imperious ringing of the front door bell. Henry opened the door as a familiar voice called, "Take the horses to the stables and be sure they are kept warm." She ran into the welcoming arms of Peregrine, who planted a brotherly kiss on her cheek.

"Perry, what are you doing here? You should be in Oxford! You haven't been sent down?"

"Such sisterly faith! No, certainly not; my tutor fully understands why I had to return home."

Henry removed the heavy caped driving coat, revealing the glory of Peregrine's attire. Georgina took in his sage-green coat with velvet collar which allowed a glimpse of striped yellow and green waistcoat. Cream leather breeches encased his slim legs and his half-length Hessian boots were tasselled. He twitched his neck cloth, demanding to know if his method of folding it the Maharatta way was not extremely taking.

"Extremely," stammered Georgina. She saw the glint of a small emerald ring and remembered he had called instructions about horses. Since the reduction in their fortunes Peregrine had travelled by mail coach, the money held in trust for him not being sufficient to maintain his own carriage, and she asked tentatively, "Did you bring home a friend, Perry?"

He gave a snort of laughter. "A fine fellow you must think me, to command a friend to stable his cattle. Oh, I know you are worrying yourself about my style of dress and travel. You needn't. I have famous news. Mama will need her hartshorn."

"Perry! You haven't married!"

"Good heavens, no! I'm under age, am I not? Better than that, George. No longer do I have to listen to a sour-faced attorney telling me I must win some rich spinster glad to marry a penniless man. Wait till you hear . . ."

But Perry flung open the morning-room door and made an entrance which gained the amazed shrieks he desired. Mrs. Havard half rose, then sank back into her chair, where she had been endeavouring to regain her composure. "My dear, dear boy. We did not expect you. How have you contrived to be here?"

He kissed her and turned to Penelope. "No welcome from you, little sister?"

She fluttered a languid hand. "Of course I am delighted to see you, Peregrine, but I am so out of sorts today."

"You, too. Georgina don't look so fit either, and Mama seems out of countenance. What's amiss here?"

"Well might you ask," cried Mrs. Havard, "but first you need refreshment, I am sure."

"Thank you ma'am. I lay last night at an inn and breakfasted at dawn so as to drive right here without a change of horses. It took much forbearance to go so slowly, I can tell you, but I could not resist showing you my beautiful new greys and a curricle watch which is a miracle of building."

His mother stared. "Curricle! Greys! And your attire! It is all new. You did not come by that in Oxford."

"Oxford? No, indeed, I have been this week in London, and I tell you, mama, there is no longer a need for you all to moulder here. They shall have their chances."

"My dearest boy, pray do not keep us in suspense. What can you mean?"

Peregrine savoured the wide-eyed attention of his womenfolk as he said, "I have taken a house for you."

"A house," shrieked Mrs. Havard, then clinging in spite of her amazement to long-held patterns of behaviour, finished, "Where is it?"

She smiled with relief as he answered impatiently, "In Upper Brook Street. Do you take me for a ninny who would rent in the wrong quarter of London? And the sooner you repair to it the better. The Season will be upon us, and you will wish to engage dressmakers. No wish to be rude, but my sisters aren't exactly gowned in the latest style."

"Oh, you are so right, my dear son, but all we have are the Misses Tomkins."

"I do sympathise, Mama, but now you can all dress up to snuff and entertain. We'll manage one whole Season, and if Penelope is not betrothed at the end of it, it won't be my fault. And as for Georgina . . ."

He looked at her and saw her staring at him with a mixture of astonishment and worry. Her frown and sitting in a draught did nothing to improve her looks. "Yes, well, I'm sure Georgina will meet someone to appreciate her true worth."

"But, Perry!" Mrs. Havard's plump cheeks were quivering with excitement, "how have you contrived to bring this about?"

"Yes, pray do tell us." Georgina's voice was tense, and her brother laughed at her. "No need for cross looks and your cold voice. All is above board, as the saying goes. This fellow, Bather, at Oxford, you know, held some shares in a Lottery Ticket. He had incurred an expense he did not wish his father to discover and needed extra blunt—a certain lady —well, we needn't go into that. The fact is, he was desperate and offered to sell me his shares. I bought, more in a desire to help him than anything. They took all the cash I could raise—Lottery Tickets don't come cheap—and the next thing I knew they had drawn several prizes and the money came to me."

Mrs. Havard seized on the fact most vital to her. "How much?" she asked simply.

"Three thousand pounds. Now what have you to say to that?"

After a few speechless seconds Mrs. Havard sank back into her cushions and gasped, "Three thousand pounds! Can this be true? I had no notion it was possible to gain so much in a lottery. Three thousand pounds! Oh, come here, my dear son, and allow your mama to kiss you."

Peregrine accepted her embrace with the caution due to his cravat.

"Ring the bell, Georgina. Your brother requires refreshment." She turned to Penelope, whose eyes were shining. "Only think, my love, we shall spend the coming Season in London. I must consult with friends to discover the modiste in fashion at present. And we must have hats—shoes, too. Oh, there is so much needing attention. Oh, why does not someone answer the bell?"

Georgina, with heightened colour said, "Because I have not yet rung it. Please allow me to speak."

"Very well, but be quick about it. I must see Webster—and Creevy. Perry, what shall we do about the carriage? It is so old and not at all the thing . . ."

Peregrine frowned. "I do not think we can purchase a new carriage. We will have the old one refurbished—it must answer for the present."

"If I may speak, Mama," ventured Georgina again.

"Oh, yes, you have something to say, I collect." Mrs. Havard's expression softened. "Do not fear, my love, I shall contrive to dress you in a becoming way."

"Mama, Perry," begged Georgina, "do but consider. If we used this money to answer some of the needs of the estate, our people would benefit and in the end our income be increased. I have heard you say these many times that a good bailiff and a capital sum would . . ." Her voice faltered as she encountered three indignant pairs of eyes.

"*If* that is all you have to say," grated her mother, "I will thank you to ring, as I requested."

Georgina capitulated. She had felt compelled to speak, knowing it would be useless. Later she requested a few words in private with her brother, and they repaired to the library which, being used only by Georgina and the governess, was unheated and smelled of mouldering leather. Peregrine smiled at his sister. "I know what you are about to say, George."

"It was nothing about the estates, though I still believe I am right."

"You were about to ask me if our mutual Papa's gambling fever ran in my veins, were you not?"

"Oh, Perry, I know I seem dismal to Mama and Penelope, and to you too, probably, but I cannot help it. Sometimes I feel so bewildered by life. Mama and Penelope seem to think only of how to contrive another gown. I love them, but I care for the poor, too, and now . . ."

Peregrine lifted her chin with a finger, "And now, little sister, you feel I have added to your burdens by winning a large sum of money."

She smiled faintly. "Put like that, I do sound foolish . . ."

"George, I swear to you, that our Papa's gambling sickness does not taint me. Of course I play for stakes, as who does not, but I have no inclination to throw away my money. I really was trying to help my friend, you know. Was it my fault I won?"

Forgetting his carefully contrived careless hairstyle he ran a hand through his curls making them stand on end. It reminded Georgina so forcibly of his boyhood, she laughed. "Oh, Perry, I am so relieved."

"And you will not hate to go to London?"

"Of course not. I am sincere in my belief in freedom for my sex, but I can still be gay."

"Now if that isn't like a female! You are inconsistent as them all, my girl."

As he held open the door for her he said quietly, "I did offer to share the win with Bather, but he would not touch it. Said I had won fair and square."

Georgina stood on tiptoe to kiss his cheek before joining the others. Her entrance was unnoticed by Mrs. Havard and Penelope, who were happily writing lists so she retired to her room and, huddled in a shawl, tried to concentrate on Mr. Buchan's advice on the care of infants, while attempting to ignore her jumbled confusion of desires in which nobility of purpose battled with her longings for a taste of fun.

During the next week Mrs. Havard drove everyone to distraction by her conflicting orders. The atmosphere was complicated by the arrival of a man of supreme dignity. He was identified as Bendish, Peregrine's new valet, and he made it insultingly plain that the Havard household was a let-down to one as lofty as he. He let it be known that had his former gentleman not left for India where he refused to accompany him, not liking foreign parts, he would not be out of a place.

From Henry Georgina learned that when the haughty valet had learned that his young master was almost untutored in London ways, and was eager to accept advice, he became devoted to him.

The journey to London was accomplished in a day, Mrs. Havard pretending not to hear the remarks of the ostler at the first posting inn when he saw their horses. They arrived in Upper Brook Street to find that the house was not large, but handsome and distinctive in appearance and well-appointed. Mrs. Havard had been busy writing letters and a gratifying number of cards were waiting. After studying these, partaking of a light supper, and meeting with the house servants, they retired for the night.

The following days were busy with fittings, choosing hats, shoes, dainty boots, reticules, and several of the enormous muffs recently in fashion.

Their first engagements were quiet ones, but as London filled the parties began, and Georgina found herself in all the bustle of the Season. One of Mrs. Havard's first tasks had been to engage the services of a dance master, upon the recommendation of her friend, Lady Sarah Knight, who explained that as he was an aristocratic refugee from the Revolution he knew how to treat young ladies with decorum. When Lady Sarah invited them to her first ball of the year, they were well prepared.

Penelope, ravishing in a white silk dress, lightly flounced and with just enough spangles to avoid vulgarity, her golden

hair entwined with tiny pearls and real flowers, was an immediate success. Mrs. Havard, arrayed in tobacco-brown
shot-silk, was thrilled to see the amazed delight on the faces
of the gentlemen presented to her younger daughter.

Georgina had refused to wear white, and not all the pleading of her mama, the tight-lipped disapproval of Webster, or
the scandalised insistence of the modiste that all young unmarried ladies wore white for evening balls, had moved her.

"I look frightful in dead white, as you well know," she
said, so in the end a compromise was reached, and she wore
a cream under-dress with an over tunic of pale green muslin.
She drew her hair back in a tight Grecian knot, from which
a few wayward curls strayed over her forehead, and Mrs.
Havard sighed.

"She seems to have no idea how to make the best of herself," she complained to Lady Sarah, "but perhaps it will
not signify. I well remember how Fanny Wylmot seemed
plain to us and how amazed we were when she made such a
dazzling match."

Lady Sarah was a kindly woman who forebore to remind
her friend that the Wylmots were so wealthy it was rumoured they had forgotten how many properties they
owned. She introduced Georgina to a stout young man, who
led her into a country dance. He had no breath for talking,
and Georgina was too busy concentrating on her steps to
care. When the dance ended, he led her back to her mother
and abandoned her with a brief bow.

She was then left tapping her feet longingly and watching
Penelope. The late arrival of Miss Ingram created a diversion. Georgina was irritated to see that as she made stately
progress around the room, greeting her many acquaintances,
Peregrine's eyes followed her with unconcealed admiration.

When he recalled that Georgina had met the beauty, he insisted they stroll casually about till they met the lady and she
was forced to make an introduction. He claimed from Miss
Ingram the two dances which propriety permitted and spent

the remainder of the evening watching her, to the annoyance of several young damsels who had eyed his tall, slender attractions with hopeful favour.

Couples were forming for a Cotillion, and suddenly Georgina realised that someone was asking for the pleasure of her company in the dance. It was too late to conceal her delight when she realised that her proposed partner was Lord Rivington. Her cheeks flaming, she began to make her excuses, then caught her mama's eye. Her hesitation cost her the chance to refuse, so she rose, laid a hand upon his arm, and suffered him to lead her on to the floor.

As they waited to begin the steps she met his steady gaze. He leaned toward her. "May I be allowed to compliment you upon your appearance, Miss Havard. You are looking particularly well."

"Thank you, sir," she answered, stifling the impulse to retort that she was not the least bit interested in his opinion, which in any case she was sure he had formed maliciously, remembering the contrast she had presented on their first meeting.

When the movement of the dance carried them apart, she gave herself up to the pleasure of the rhythm, and when next they came together, he smiled, "You dance most gracefully."

"Thank you, sir," she said again. Not for worlds would she give him the opportunity to ridicule her. She could only suppose that his asking her to take the floor indicated his boredom both with the evening and the many girls panting for his notice, and his desire for some sport at her expense.

When she noticed that several young bucks were ogling her through their eye-glasses, she gritted her teeth in rage. They were laughing among themselves and she wondered if they were wagering how long it would be before the Earl provoked her into saying something unbecoming. She did not doubt that he and Miss Ingram had primed their friends to expect original behaviour from the eccentric Miss Georgina Havard.

By looking away from him whenever they were near she managed to complete the dance without giving him an opportunity to speak again. He led her back to her mother and she was about to sink thankfully on to a bench when she was furious to hear him asking her mama's consent to take her to the refreshment room.

Drowning Georgina's protestations, her mother cried, "How delightfully kind and thoughtful of you, my lord. I declare Georgina does look a little flushed."

Georgina had no alternative but to rise and once more place her hand upon Lord Rivington's arm and pace beside him from the ballroom. They were followed by the malevolent stares of mothers and daughters, who speculated upon what this unappealing looking woman possessed to attract the Earl. Mrs. Havard's plump face was almost contorted by her effort to remain placid in the gaze of society and not reveal her gratification that one of the world's most eligible beaux paid her child this signal attention. Inwardly she prayed that the unpredictable girl would do or say nothing to disgrace her family.

At the refreshment table, which was laden with numbers of tempting dishes, the Earl bowed and asked Georgina what she would take.

"Nothing, I thank you," she replied through stiff lips. "You must be well aware that I accompanied you only because of Mama. I consider your behaviour to be shameful in the light of what previously passed between us."

Lord Rivington gave a smile which contained no amusement. "Are you referring to our encounter in the woods, my dear Miss Havard, or to my later apology?"

Georgina flushed. He had said he was sorry, yet his every action toward her made her more certain that he was mocking her, simply using her to amuse himself.

"I am not your 'dear Miss Havard,' " she said, "and I think it ungentlemanly of you even to remember that first meeting leave alone to mention it."

"You are so right. You are not my 'dear Miss Havard'

and I presume too far, yet I fear I cannot forget an incident which though shaming me to recall also brings with it a memory of a quite delightful contact and a rejection of the most spirited kind."

She looked up to see his elegant hand caress the cheek she had struck and saw an expression in his laughing grey eyes which made her heart beat faster. Could she be mistaken in her opinion of him? She searched his face to try to fathom what lay behind the facade, and all the delicacy and humanity of her compassionate nature were written clearly in that look.

He caught his breath and held out his hand. "Miss Havard, I . . ."

"Good evening, my dear Rivington. Do pray introduce me to this young lady. She must indeed be fascinating to have made you forget your manners."

The Earl swore beneath his breath as he turned to the man who had interrupted them. "My manners?"

"Yes, indeed, for Miss Ingram is tapping her foot more in temper than in rhythm as she waits for you to lead her into the dance which is just beginning. Alas, she refuses to accept me as substitute."

Lord Rivington turned a cold demeanour on Georgina as he gave a formal bow. "Miss Havard, allow me to present you to my cousin, Sir Francis Calland, Francis this is . . ."

"No need to continue, dear cousin, I believe I know the identity of the lady. I collect she must be the one of whom I have heard so much, so do hurry to your impatient partner and leave me to amuse our budding lady physician."

Georgina's angry flush was not missed by either man as Rivington left them and returned to the ballroom. Sir Francis gave her a sympathetic look. "Allow me to offer you a glass of champagne punch. So refreshing! Then you shall tell me the truth about yourself. I was amused when I heard the tales being circulated, but having met you I perceive you are a woman of distinction."

"I wonder you care to be seen with me at all," said Georgina, stiffly. "I can well imagine what you must have heard of me."

She glanced at the doorway through which the Earl had just walked, and Sir Francis gave a gentle smile. "He was not the only one at Kennerley, you know. There were others, you should remember."

She warmed to a man who would defend his cousin knowing him to be indefensible.

"I have long felt," he continued, "that women are held captive by foolish bonds of convention. I am truly interested in your views."

Georgina expanded beneath his charm. He was almost as tall as the Earl, but more slender. His eyes were a curious contrast with his dark brown hair, being a very light blue-grey, and as Georgina talked he fixed them on her and listened to her more attentively than anyone except Luke Musgrove had ever done. She was enchanted by him.

He danced twice with her, and other young bucks, curious to discover how she could attract Rivington and his cousin, began to pay her attention—and she scarcely sat down for the rest of the evening.

CHAPTER 5

"A most successful ball," pronounced Mrs. Havard the following day, as they breakfasted late. "Penelope, I really believe that Sir Stannard is smitten. And you, Georgina, I declare I was most gratified . . ." She broke off, recognising that to express amazement that her eldest daughter should have been asked to dance so often was hardly flattering.

Georgina, who was feeling unaccountably low in spirits, answered her mother briefly.

Mrs. Havard was anxious. "You are not ill, my love?"

"No, Mama, only tired, I think." Once she would have felt touched by her mother's concern for her health, but today she could not care.

"Did you feel any particularity for any of the gentlemen, Georgina?"

"I found Sir Francis Calland a most . . . most interesting companion."

Mrs. Havard was sharp. "That one is not to be encouraged. It is true that he is Rivington's heir, but the Earl is in abounding health and likely to marry and produce many healthy offspring, so there is nothing to be hoped for there. And he has gone through the fortune left him by his father and is now deep in debt In fact, I understand that his income derives solely from a generous allowance paid him by the Earl and that it should be enough for any man of fashion, but Sir Francis . . ."

"I have no doubt," interrupted Georgina coldly, "that any scurrilous tales about him can have only one source and that is his cousin, the great Alexander Rivington. Please excuse me, Mama, I do have the headache, and think I will lie down."

"Do so," agreed Mrs. Havard, "but do not forget that later today we are to visit Madame Hachette for the fitting of your court gown. And then I must decide to whom we should apply for our vouchers for Almacks. It will not do for us not to be seen there. We might as well have stayed at home."

Penelope, who was one of the fortunates whose beauty was simply enhanced by faint blue shadows of weariness beneath her eyes, yawned and said languidly, "Sir Stannard will not be put off by my not attending Almacks surely, Mama."

Her mother frowned "You never can tell with gentlemen,

dearest. Even the most enamoured of them can draw back with alarming haste if they believe that the object of their affections is not fully accepted into society."

Penelope's sleepiness was replaced by alarm. "Then we *must* have the vouchers! I could not bear to return home without having secured a betrothal, I could not . . ." Her eyes filled with tears, and her mother patted her hand.

"Do not fret. I fancy my influence still holds in places."

But the worried lines stayed between her eyes. Two years was a long time to be away, and Mr. Havard had left debts. She didn't consider those of the tradesmen, who had begun to cluster round as soon as she reappeared on the scene, but she was by no means certain that her late husband had not borrowed from friends. And God knew what tales might be circulating about Georgina. Only let the patronesses of Almacks decide against them, and their chances of obtaining the coveted vouchers would disappear.

Georgina slowly climbed the stairs to her bed chamber. She had begun to wish they had never left their country home. There at least, in spite of the daily irritation of her mother's grumbles and the necessary shifts of economy, she knew her world. She could rise in the mornings and go out among people whose needs and ways she understood. There she was not forced into the company of a society behind whose smiling eyes and gentle tongues lurked twin serpents of mockery and torment.

She remembered that tonight they were to go to the theatre to see the famous Mr. Kemble and Mrs. Siddons in a new production of *Macbeth*. Once the idea would have made her feel ecstatic, but now she found her pleasure spoiled. Irritation quickened her steps, and she almost collided with her brother as he left his room.

"Beg your pardon, George," he said, giving her a bow which would have done credit to a court drawing room. He was dressed, as always these days, in the height of fashion, but his new coat of superfine blue cloth and looped tricot breeches appeared to be giving him little satisfaction, if his expression was anything to judge. Georgina looked with concern at the worried frown which sat unfamiliarly on his usually placid face and caught his arm. "Perry, is anything amiss?"

He removed her hand gently, saying, "Dearest Georgina, do not, I beg, clutch at my coat in that manner." He smiled down at her. "Such a foolish little sister you are, to concern yourself with my problems. 'Tis nothing, I assure you."

Georgina turned to leave, unconvinced, then paused as he asked, "Is Mama still talking of your court dresses?"

At her nod, he frowned deeper. "Damned expensive things, ain't they? Beg your pardon, George. I suppose it is absolutely necessary for a girl to be presented? Yes, of course it is. Stupid question. Don't know why I asked it. Well, I must be off. Arranged to meet Kennerley. Cockfight, you know."

Georgina watched him run lightly downstairs, a feeling of apprehension tugging at her, then she went into her room and sat watching the passing traffic in the street below.

Apart from the visit to Madame Hachette, where Mrs. Havard demanded, and was promised, the finest materials and trimmings for the girls' court dresses, Georgina spent the day quietly, declining to drive out with her mother and sister.

"It is so provoking that we have no carriage fit to be seen in," complained Mrs. Havard, "but fortunately Lady Sarah is calling for us. Do come, Georgina, you look positively hagged. I am persuaded that a visit to the delightful shops in Bond Street would restore your spirits. Oh, very well, if you won't. But I am sure that moping at home will do nothing to help your looks."

She left, frowning, but returned some time later bursting with news. "Never again shall we lumber to the theatre and balls in that unsprung horror which masquerades as our carriage," she declared gleefully, "for Lady Sarah has a friend who is retiring from London for the sake of her husband's health. Only imagine, Georgina, she recently purchased a town coach and has allowed us to buy it at much below its original price. She will be living outside the town of Weymouth and will have no use for a light vehicle. Poor soul, she looked quite put out, though it is a lucky affair for us."

"Yes, and we settled at once," cried Penelope, "and arrived home in fine style. I tell you, I almost laughed to see the butler's face when he opened the door and saw us return in a carriage with double steps, red silk festoon curtains, and our own coachman."

"You have engaged a coachman, too? What about Creevy? Can he not drive us? Whatever will Perry say to this added expense?"

"Oh, he will be delighted," laughed Penelope. "He can hardly set himself up in the forefront of fashion and expect his womenfolk to trundle around in an eighteenth-century carriage."

Mrs. Havard's frown returned as she glared at her eldest daughter. "If that is not exactly like you, Georgina, to try to dampen our spirits. The coachman would have been turned off if we had not taken him on, so you must agree that I performed an act of charity there. Also Creevy is old and needs help."

"Besides, the new coachman is young and has elegant calves," giggled Penelope.

"That will do, miss!" ordered Mrs. Havard. "Such talk from a young lady. All the same, she is right. He goes with the carriage so that is settled. As do the horses," she added.

"You have bought horses, too?"

"Pray tell of what use would a coach be without?"

"Why none at all, ma'am, but they can be hired."

"Mama is right," cried Penelope, "you must always be spoiling our pleasure. You are determined to be disagreeable."

"I beg your pardon," said Georgina quietly, "I have no

wish to act unpleasantly. In any case, the thing seems to be done, and we must hope that Peregrine sees it in the same light as you."

Her brother returned soon after, looking flushed and triumphant, and bringing Sir Francis with him. Mrs. Havard, who secretly felt she had been rash in her purchases decided to break her news to him while Sir Francis talked to the girls, feeling that Peregrine could scarcely create a scene with company present.

To her relief, he laughed loudly. "You're a rare one, Mama. Only fancy bringing such a thing off by yourself. What think you of my mother, Calland?"

As he related the story Georgina realised that his speech was slurred and suspected that he had been drinking heavily besides being in a high state of excitement.

"While you have been spending the family fortune, ladies, I have been mending it," he told them. "Sir Francis was obliging enough to tell me which of the cocks to bet on, and I have had a good day of it, I can tell you."

"Cockfighting!" shrieked Mrs. Havard. "Do not, I beg, bring talk of such horrid doings into my drawing room."

"No, indeed," agreed Sir Francis smoothly, "ladies do not, in general, care for such subjects. Do you attend the theatre tonight? There is much talk of the new production of *Macbeth*."

"We do, indeed. Perry, why do you not accompany us?"

She had spoken without thought, knowing Peregrine's dislike of what he termed "ranting actors," and was astonished when he replied, "I was about to suggest the same idea myself, Mama. I should be pleased to escort you."

Georgina saw how uncomfortable his new friend's implied rebuke regarding cockfighting had made her brother and therefore was cool when Sir Francis bowed over her hand and murmured, "I shall look forward to seeing you tonight then, Miss Havard. I shall be sure to look for you."

"You will not have far to seek us out," said Mrs. Havard

complacently, "for we shall be in Sir Stannard Morton's own box."

"Till tonight," said Sir Francis softly, his hand holding Georgina's a little longer than was necessary. His light eyes were fixed upon her face in an expression she could not fathom. He seemed to be singling her out for attention, and she wondered if she was supposed to feel flattered. He must know that she was not an heiress, and if her mother was right about his own financial prospects, then his attitude towards her was puzzling.

And why had he taken Perry up so obviously? He was an experienced man of the world—she judged his age to be about one and thirty. Perhaps he truly liked them and would prove a steadying influence upon her brother, who certainly needed it in the heady position of finding himself in London, with money, and entirely responsible for the welfare of his womenfolk.

Eliza helped her to dress for the evening in a pale yellow gown and watched her mistress walk about the room, turning in the way the dancing master had told her would control her short train. Georgina surprised an expression on the maid's face which told her, clearer than words, that Eliza, who had lost little of her sullenness since arriving in London, considered it a waste of time to try to improve the looks of a woman whose appearance she derided and whose outlook on life she found incomprehensible. Georgina dismissed the maid and arranged her own hair in its usual style.

A knock was followed by the entrance of her brother, who surveyed his sister and said with brotherly candour, "You'll never make a beauty, love, but there's something about you if only . . . I swear you could appear to greater advantage—perhaps it's your hair."

Georgina, easing on her kid gloves, laughed. "Is my brother then an arbiter of feminine fashion?"

Peregrine grinned. "I think I know a little of it. Do you like my own attire?"

Georgina's hazel eyes were alight with mischief. "The only word for you, Perry, is—gorgeous."

He laughed, but a flush mounted his cheeks. "You don't consider I have gone too far? I assure you this is quite the thing."

Georgina surveyed her brother's handsome figure, clad in claret coat over white marcello waistcoat, cream breeches, white silk stockings and black slippers and told him he looked truly magnificent. "If I have any criticism, dear, it is only that your neck-cloth . . ."

He interrupted her with lofty disdain. "Ah, there I cannot allow a female to pretend to know anything. It is tied in a *Throne d'amour,* and I spoilt eight others in achieving the effect."

"Eight?"

"Bendish assures me that some men spoil thrice that number often. He says I have the right touch."

"I see." Georgina was demure. "If Bendish approves, then who am I to judge?"

"Tease! I've a good mind not to give you my presents, but I will. Turn about."

She obeyed him, and he slipped a pendant around her neck, fixing it for her. She looked at the delicately wrought cross in surprise as he explained, "That is the very latest in Berlin ironwork jewellery. It will make the other women envious, I think. And here is my other gift."

She opened a package to reveal a fan, which she displayed with a gasp of delight.

"I couldn't resist it," explained Peregrine, as she gently touched the leaf vellum painted in gouache. "See, the subject of the picture is 'The Drawing of a State Lottery'! So apt, don't you think? Maybe it will bring us luck. I fancy we shall need it."

She looked sharply into his face. "Perry, I cannot get it out of my head that you are worried. You would tell me, would you not, if you needed my help or advice?"

"Advice? From you, little innocent? Only be happy, George; that is all I ask of you."

She was not satisfied, but the finality of his tone told her that he would say no more. She took his hand. "You are the best of brothers to share your money so generously, when you might have kept it for yourself. And Perry, I am so glad you are to accompany us tonight, when I know that other occupations would amuse you more."

Tell-tale colour rose to her brother's cheeks. "Perry, I believe you expect to meet someone tonight. You are using us to see a lady. Tell me who! I know I must like her if you do."

"You have already met her and could not have failed to be struck by her beauty and charm."

Georgina frowned in concentration, but finally shook her head. "Do not tease me, I implore . . ."

"It is Miss Charlotte Ingram," Peregrine declared simply. "Remember you introduced us. Is she not the loveliest creature imaginable? Such grace, such fine eyes—and that glorious hair."

For an instant Georgina was speechless, then she blurted, "But so proud! Perry, how can you imagine she will look at you? Mama says she is set on marrying Lord Rivington. You cannot hope to compete with him." As memories of the Earl flooded her mind, she finished, "They will do very well together, those two."

Peregrine grasped her wrist urgently, "Georgina, I will not have you speak a word against her. In her behaviour to me she was all that was amiable and encouraging. I mean to try to win her."

Georgina said no more, but her heart was heavy as she realised how little chance her impressionable brother had with such as the Honourable Miss Ingram.

Later, as she sat entranced by the play, all disturbing thoughts were swamped. Sir Stannard Morton had dined with them, in the peacock splendour of a blue satin coat, a starched neck-cloth so high he could scarcely move his head, his pudgy hands flashing with sapphires and diamonds which caught the fire of the enormous jewel in his cravat. He spoke little and ate heartily.

Mrs. Havard had been fortunate enough to engage a chef who regarded cookery as a creative art, and Sir Stannard applied himself with enthusiasm, partaking of many dishes and paying particular attention to the Pigeons-in-Savoury-Jelly and Florendine Rabbits, and ending with liberal portions of Brandy-fruits and forced strawberries. With each course he drank generous draughts of wine, and when he was finally finished, he rose from the table with his face shining with pleasure and repletion, to offer his arm to Penelope.

Georgina sighed with admiration at her sister's looks. The soft rose colour of Penelope's satin slip exactly matched her complexion, and the Grecian overdress of white gauze flowed round her exquisite form as if in a caress. Her golden curls had been expertly dressed and now had a rose satin bow in their shining masses. A simple chain with a diamond pendant hung round her soft white neck.

Sir Stannard's box commanded a good view of the stage and the pit, where Georgina was amazed to see bejewelled dandies of all ages with painted faces, standing to ogle shamelessly any lady who caught their fancy.

Robert Kennerley came to pay his respects, as did several new acquaintances, and Mrs. Havard was gratified to find how many of her old friends welcomed her return. Penelope was in high spirits as several gentlemen prevailed upon those already known to her to present them to the new beauty, but Georgina noticed that she was careful never to say or do anything which might seem to cut out Sir Stannard.

During the second interval, as Georgina sat quietly reliving the drama so thrillingly portrayed, she realised that her mother was speaking. "Georgina, my love, here is someone to see you. I declare, you are so absorbed it is impossible to gain your attention."

Her eyes, still misty with enjoyment, failed for an instant to comprehend who was there, then a well-remembered voice said, "Good evening, Miss Havard. It's plain to see that the play finds favour with you."

"Lord Rivington! I did not expect you."

"Georgina, my dearest, remember your manners. His lordship is asking you to take a turn about the theatre with him. Boxes are so cramping, are they not, Lord Rivington, though not so much as the benches in the pit." This last was added hastily, with a beaming smile at Sir Stannard.

"I am well content here, Mama. I'm sure his lordship has other acquaintances to see."

"Nonsense! She is such a good girl—so unwilling to put herself forward like some of these modern misses—now do you go with the Earl, my love, he has been waiting some moments for you."

Georgina bit her lip, rose, and left the box. She and Lord Rivington walked slowly, until Georgina, uncomfortable at the silence, said, "What think you of the play?"

"I find it quite tolerable, thank you."

"Am I to understand, sir, that you do not care for the performance, as your tone implies?"

"I thought Mr. Kemble's Macbeth nearly perfect, and Mr. Charles Kemble is spirited as Macduff, but I found a certain unexpected languor in the performance of Mrs. Siddons."

"Of course, you would find it easy to criticize anything done by a woman!"

"Am I then not to speak the truth of what I find? It is her first attempt at the part—she has not yet settled into it—that is all I meant. She is a magnificent creature."

"I am sure she would be much obliged to you for your comment."

Georgina was obliged to stand still as Lord Rivington stopped walking. "Well, upon my word, Miss Havard, I was merely making an observation. I have only to speak to have you unsheath your sword and flash its blade before my nose. Have you no polite conversation?"

She glared into his grinning face. "I have conversation which fits the company, and I find yours so often offensive."

"Miss Havard, believe me, I do not mean it to be so. I have said how much I regret our first disastrous meeting. I have tried hard to find a level at which we may converse with pleasure."

As people returned to their seats the corridor emptied, and suddenly Lord Rivington took her hand and stepped close to her. Her heart began to pound until she felt she would suffocate as she struggled with feelings which were as unforeseen as they were startling. She had an impulse to hold tight to that strong white hand, to lean toward him and allow him to embrace her; she felt the powerful attraction of him. *He is bad; you are a fool,* she told herself. She looked into his face and for an instant their eyes met in something that seemed more than understanding. Alarmed, she snatched her hand away, saying, "You have no right! You are presumptuous!" And she hurried back to the box without looking back, yet knowing that his intense gaze followed her.

She pretended to concentrate on the players, ignoring her mother's whispered questions, until she was left in peace. But the remainder of the play was spoilt for her. She sat motionless through the farce, hearing, as if from a distance, the gales of laughter from the audience. She was glad to retire that night, but she slept only in short, restless periods as her thoughts and troubled dreams intermingled and were dominated by Alexander Rivington.

Georgina rose early and stayed in her bed-chamber by the fire, trying to concentrate on her *Book of Domestic Medicine.* She heard a maid enter her sister's room, which was opposite. Perhaps talking to Penelope would help her regain some tranquillity. She found her sister sitting up in bed, drinking hot chocolate. "Lord, Georgina, it is barely ten o'clock and you are already dressed. I declare I am quite fatigued."

"I could not sleep."

Penelope's delicate brows rose, and she straightened her lace nightcap. "Oh? You walked and talked with Lord Rivington, did you not? Did you find his conversation so stimulating?"

Georgina carefully controlled her voice. "I had forgotten that. I found the play a wonderful experience."

"Wonderful? Oh, I suppose it was. Well, of course I revere Shakespeare, as who does not? Everyone must, I know, but I find I most enjoy times when I can talk."

"I see. I feel I owe you an apology. I was so preoccupied I left you to entertain Sir Stannard and did nothing to help. He is so tedious—I compliment you on your superior behaviour, Penny."

Penelope lost her drowsiness and became flushed and animated. "I do not find him tedious," she exclaimed, her blue eyes flashing.

Georgina stammered, "Pray . . . do forgive me . . . I did not know you cared about him."

"Cared about him? What does that signify? He could come to care for me—and he is so rich that he could give me all I ever wanted. I have no intention of being buried in the country if I can help it.

"You look shocked, Georgina. Well, I suppose such remarks are not seemly." She continued slowly, "Of course, I would not marry only for money—do not think it—but Mama has explained that married love is only for the vulgar masses. And in any case I have not yet had time to develop a tendre for Sir Stannard. And if I did, it would be forward of me when he has not yet declared himself. But I could learn to care for him, of that I am sure."

"You relieve my mind," said Georgina bleakly. She had watched Sir Stannard and did not doubt that he would offer for her sister. She disliked the idea of having him for a

brother, but if she followed her plan to marry Luke Musgrove and work with him, Sir Stannard would probably ignore her existence. She rose abruptly and startled Penelope,
who was sipping her chocolate and staring pensively ahead.

"Georgina! Must you be so sudden? Here, I have spilt
chocolate on my new night gown. Ring for a maid at once, I
beg."

Georgina did so and went back to her room. The day was
fine, though chilly, and she decided that a brisk walk might
clear her mind. She pulled her fur-lined mantle about her
and considered ringing for Eliza to accompany her, but the
memory of the girl's sullen face stopped her. I need to be
alone anyway, she thought. So, pulling her hood over her
head, she slipped out and made her way to Hyde Park.

The park looked intensely green in the cool sunshine of
early spring and she drew a deep breath of pure pleasure,
realising how cramped she sometimes felt in the city. Walking along, she tried to see the past weeks in perspective. She,
who had prided herself on the logic of her mind, could make
no sense of her jumbled emotions. She thought of Perry and
wondered how he was faring in this new life. He seemed to
have responded with almost feverish eagerness to the demands made on a fashionable young buck, and lately Sir
Francis Calland always made up one of his party. She could
not suppose that it was usual for a man of his mature years
to sponsor one so young and inexperienced and wondered
where lay the attraction.

In her absorption she did not at first realise that she was
being accosted by a strange young man astride a spirited
grey. He swept off his hat and gave her a bow as low as
could be accomplished from the back of a horse.

She paused. Possibly she had met him at some party and
forgotten him. Turning her clear eyes to him, she said,
"Good morning, sir. You have the advantage of me, I fear."

He looked startled, mumbled something indistinguishable
about "a mistake" and trotted quickly away. For a moment

she was astonished at such behaviour. Then, as she looked about her, it occurred to her that she might have been less than wise to walk alone in a London park. She saw a few nurses with their charges, one or two shawled women hurrying about their business, but most numerous were gentlemen exercising their mounts.

However irritated she might feel at the limitations imposed upon the behaviour of ladies in the city, she decided she must accept them and began to hurry toward the park entrance.

As she walked she passed two young women, both of whom looked pale and undernourished and were dressed in clothes which had been many times patched and mended. The younger of the two carried a child in a ragged shawl, and they stared at her as she hastened by. There was no animosity in their gaze. There was nothing, Georgina realised, but a kind of hopeless blankness, as if they looked without seeing.

Her impulse was to stop, but she had not brought her reticule and could offer them no money. Even if she could have, she was not at all sure how one went about giving charity to strangers. It was all so different at home.

She walked swiftly on and was now horribly conscious of the attention she was drawing from some of the horsemen. She heard exclamations from a couple of grooms, which she felt thankful she could not understand.

Suddenly there was the sound of a loud altercation behind her. She paused, began to walk again, then stopped as she heard a female voice shrill in distress. "She did not touch your purse, sir. If it is gone from your pocket, then you must have lost it somewhere."

The voice was drowned by others, all dominated by the bull-like roar of a man. Georgina turned and saw the two pale young women cowering beneath the waving arms of a portly red-cheeked man whose sober dress proclaimed him a merchant. He was being vociferously encouraged by a shrew-faced woman and several noisy children.

Seeing a woman in trouble was enough to send Georgina running back. "What's the trouble here?"

She was forced to repeat herself very loudly before the whole company stopped yelling to look at her.

The man explained in a bullying country accent, "I've bin robbed, that's what the trouble is. I'd a roll of bills in my pocket until that wench carrying the child fell against me. Pretending to be in a swoon she was, but I've bin warned of her sort before I came here, and my hand went straight away to my pocket to find it empty." He turned it inside out as if to prove his point.

The older girl, holding the half-fainting figure of her companion and trying to support the baby, said piteously, "Indeed, sir, my friend did not—would not—we are honest maids, sir."

The man's wife shrilled, "Haul her before a magistrate, William, and have her put away. Her sort shouldn't be allowed to roam abroad preying on honest folk."

The children agreed shriekingly with their parent, and Georgina gave up trying to make herself heard and spoke to the young woman. "What ails your friend?"

"Naught but hunger, miss. We'm both hungry, but stealing is what we'd never stoop to, I swear."

The big man thrust out his arm and grasped Georgina by the shoulder. "Thieves they be, and I don't doubt you're in with 'em. You'll all come along with me and . . ."

The rest of his speech was lost in a bellow of rage as he found himself in the grip of an iron hand which dragged him away from Georgina and sent him staggering. "What the hell . . . ?"

"Your language is as appalling before ladies as your manners," said an icy voice. Georgina turned to find herself staring at Lord Rivington.

"Oh, thank God you are come, sir. Please tell this man that these girls are innocent of theft."

"That has yet to be proved," was the cold reply, and at that the merchant's face brightened.

"I beg pardon, sir, if my natural indignation outran my manners . . ."

"It did," said the Earl, and the man fell silent.

"If this girl truly has stolen your money, perhaps you will tell me where she has hidden it."

"Somewhere about her person," shrieked the merchant's wife, then encountering a look from his lordship's cold grey eyes, she too was quiet.

"Did you take this man's money?" asked the Earl of the elder girl.

"No, we did not," she replied, "and we are ready to be searched here and now."

Lord Rivington addressed Georgina, "Miss Havard, if you will be so good . . ."

"Of course," she responded, but before she could begin the red-faced man cried, "How can you know she ain't in a conspiracy with 'em? She was quick enough on the scene."

Slowly Lord Rivington's slender fingers slid down the ribbon of his eye-glass. Equally slowly he raised it to survey the merchant, whose face went several shades redder as he spluttered, "Beg your pardon. I meant no offence. But how was I to know? I saw this woman—lady," he hastily amended, as the Earl felt once more for his glass, "and she was walking unattended in the park. Well, what I say is . . ."

"You say a deal too much," said his lordship. "Miss Havard, be so good, please . . ."

He waved a languid hand toward the two young women, and Georgina rapidly examined their clothing. "No money here," she said briefly.

"What about the baby?" rasped the merchant's wife. "They could have slipped something there."

The young mother's eyes were closed, but her face went whiter. "As if I would," she murmured weakly, but Georgina rapidly searched the tiny form and shook her head.

The merchant began to bluster. "Well, what I say is, it's a fine thing if a man can't walk in a London park without being robbed of . . . that is to say, losing his money. Come on, Jane, let's leave . . ."

"A moment more of your time, I beg," said Lord Rivington. "You have made a serious accusation against these two women. Be so good as to examine your own person for the missing bills. Or must I do it for you." His voice became abruptly harsh as the man hesitated, then hastily slid his hand into one after another of his pockets. His face turned puce as he reluctantly withdrew a fat roll of bills.

"Anyone can make a mistake," he spluttered.

"A mistake which might have led to the apprehension on a serious charge of two innocent females," pointed out Lord Rivington, "perhaps even three," he added, throwing Georgina an unfathomable look. "You owe them an apology."

"Apology," screamed the merchant's wife. "I'd have you know that my husband is rich and respected where we come from, and not in the habit of apologizing to ragbag women like these two."

"So I should suppose." Lord Rivington's voice was icily contemptuous. "Nevertheless, I think an apology is needed here."

Spluttering with anger, the merchant expressed his "sorrow" and led his vociferous wife and brood away.

Lord Rivington turned to Georgina, and his voice was now glacial. "Allow me to escort you home, madam, since you have seen fit to dispense with the attendance of a servant."

Her warm gratitude for his help vanished, and she longed to refuse, yet her innate honesty recognised the propriety of his offer. But she could not admit her need so easily. He was in riding dress and she stammered, "W . . . what about your horse?"

"My friend will lead him to his stable. How remiss of me, but in the exigencies of the situation I have forgot my manners—pray allow me to present to you Mr. Anthony Briton. He has been out of town, so you will not previously have met."

A horseman who had been watching the scene from a distance reined forward and slid to the ground. Georgina found herself looking into brown eyes which were alight with sympathy and laughter before he made his bow. She responded with a curtsey. "I am truly sorry to put you both to such trouble, but really I cannot leave the park without first enquiring into the circumstances of these poor girls. Please bear with me for a while."

Mr. Briton's generous response was cut short by the Earl. "Anthony, please find out where these women may be found and I will send them help. Does that satisfy you, madam? And now, since you have exposed yourself to insult enough for one day, you will please to accompany me—now!"

CHAPTER 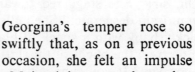 Georgina's temper rose so swiftly that, as on a previous occasion, she felt an impulse to strike at this arrogant man. Maintaining control over her itching fingers, she stared at him, and his eyes met and locked with hers. She despised the way her voice shook a little as she said, "Sir, you have no right . . . I am truly grateful for your intervention just now, but that does not give you leave to . . ."

"It is scarcely a question of right, Miss Havard. You will perhaps allow that it is at it's best, foolish, at worst, improper, of you to be walking unattended in a public park."

"Improper! How dare you! How could I know . . . ?"

"A moment's intelligent thought would have convinced

you. You pride yourself, I collect, on being a woman of brains rather than . . ."

He stopped, and Georgina felt a little sick. Was his next word going to have been "beauty"? Surely he could not humiliate her so in front of strangers. She fought to regain control over herself. What did it matter what this hateful man thought of her?

"I will not leave here until I have spoken with these two poor creatures," she declared. "If you do not pity their plight, then allow me to do so."

The women had drawn apart and stood in a hopeless huddle beneath a tree, the younger leaning against the trunk with eyes still closed and a face now as waxen as death.

Mr. Briton, who had been watching his friend and the young lady with a good deal of interest, interposed. "They do look done up. Surely there could be no harm in allowing her to enquire into their circumstances, Rivington. A woman's touch, you know."

His voice carried clearly on the bright morning air, and at the sound of it the eyes of the young mother flew open wide. "Rivington," she repeated. "Is it truly my lord Rivington? Oh, sir!" She staggered toward him, "I must speak with you. I am desperate." She pulled aside the shawl, revealing a sickly baby with a shock of black curls. "Can you look unmoved on the plight of this little one who surely has a claim upon you? If you cannot help me, then help him—in God's name, do not turn us away."

Mr. Briton stood perfectly still. In other circumstances Georgina could have laughed at the picture of utter consternation he presented. "Rivington," he gasped, "my dear fellow—I do apologise—I am at a loss for words."

The Earl looked at him coldly. "Then pray continue to be so. Take Miss Havard away from here, if you please. I wish to speak privately with this girl."

Mr. Briton hastily tethered the horses and held out an arm. Wordlessly Georgina placed cold fingertips upon it and they walked briskly from the scene toward the park entrance.

"No wonder he wanted me to go," said Georgina, with a sob in her voice. "That poor abandoned woman and her child. Of course, he must have recognised her as soon as he looked properly at her, though it is hardly surprising he did not know her instantly. She looks to be at death's door, and I daresay she used to be pretty when first they met."

"My dear madam," protested Mr. Briton, "do not, I beg, leap to conclusions which are likely to be entirely false. If, as you say, he knew her, then why did he not allow her to be arrested for theft? That would have removed her effectively from his path."

"How can I tell what were his motives? Perhaps he feared that she would tell a magistrate of his perfidy and there would be—unpleasantness for him."

"I cannot believe that my friend would treat a woman so. Have you considered that she might be creating a scandal in the hopes that someone will pay her to go away. There are such women, you know."

Georgina stopped, and he received the full benefit of the flashing beauty of her furious eyes. "She was too ill to be pretending. You know it—and so do I. How could he act so?"

"Beg pardon, miss."

The voice was soft and they saw that they had been caught up by the elder of the two women. "His lordship is talking with my friend, Queeney, and has sent me with a message. Please will Mr. Briton escort the young lady home, then send a groom to fetch the horses, and as soon as possible he wants his travelling coach to be sent here, prepared for a journey to his Berkshire estates and food and wine placed aboard."

Mr. Briton's face went pink as he avoided Georgina's eyes. "I will do all he asks," he said, a shade too heartily, "no doubt he has taken pity on your friend, my good young woman, and desires to help her."

His voice dwindled before their combined stare and he once more held out his arm to Georgina. She spoke to the girl. "Pray what plans has his lordship for you?"

"Why none, miss. I have been told that I may safely leave Queeney in his care. I must find work."

She sighed and drew the patched shawl about her painfully thin body.

"What do you do?"

"If it please you, miss, I am a seamstress. Leastways I was till I was turned off."

"And will you be able to obtain further employment?"

The girl flushed. "I don't rightly know, me being not as strong as I was." As if to give credence to her words, she staggered and clutched at Georgina's arm for support. "I . . . I beg pardon, miss. I haven't eaten for . . . for a long while."

Georgina turned to Mr. Briton. "You may be about Lord Rivington's business, sir. This young person will be my escort to my home. I shall at least make sure she eats today.'·

Mr. Briton's eyes were troubled. "I believe I should not allow it, but . . ." He looked back to where the Earl was still in conversation with the girl. "If you are sure . . ."

"Perfectly, thank you. Now come, my dear, I will take you home with me."

Safely home, she helped the young woman to her bed-chamber and seated her before the fire, then rang for refreshment to be brought.

Eliza goggled her astonishment. "You've brought that . . . that female in off the streets. Whatever will your mother say?"

"Please convey my wishes to the kitchen staff," said Georgina coldly. "I shall not ask for your further assistance."

The famished girl wolfed the bread and soup provided and sipped the hot milk. A little colour stole into her face, and Georgina saw that she was quite pretty. She told of her circumstances in halting tones, her voice often thickened by tears. "I'm Jenny Marsh, if you please, miss, and was happy as a farmer's daughter till a fever carried off my parents and brother in under a week. Being as we were only tenants, I had to leave the farm and come to London. I've always had an ability with my needle, so I hired myself as a seamstress."

"That seems a sensible line of conduct to have taken," said Georgina gently. "What went wrong?"

"Well, miss," answered Jenny slowly, "it might make you angry telling you of these things, you being one of the gentry folk who benefit by our work, but it isn't right what those women have to suffer. We slaved all hours round the clock, with almost no victuals, and on Sundays wandered around with no food at all. The masters don't allow work on the Sabbath, you see, so we got turned out of doors from dawn to dark and our wages being so small we couldn't buy even a crust to keep us going. Then when there's a wedding or a funeral, the sewing women must keep on."

She stopped for a moment, then her eyes darkened as she continued, "There was a grand wedding and we had only eight hours sleep in three days and not near enough food. I swooned and master said it hadn't to happen again—he said it wasted my time—and besides when I fell I pricked my finger and a drop of blood fell on a piece of silk and master said I should pay for it. I tried hard to keep going, but it was no good—I swooned twice more. The other women covered for me the first time, but they couldn't keep hiding me, so I was turned off without a penny because I owed for the silk."

Georgina listened with mounting horror to these revelations. She sprang to her feet, pacing the room, her eyes sparkling with indignation.

"You shall tell me where this slave shop is to be discovered. I will speak to a magistrate—this cannot be allowed to continue."

"But, miss, they're all like that. Leastways all the ones

I've seen, though I heard that some masters are good. Why, that very dress you wear now . . ." She stopped, flushing deeply. "Oh, miss, I shouldn't have said that . . . you weren't to know . . . and you so kind to me . . ."

Georgina looked down at her delicately worked gown and plucked it nervously, "I didn't know—I had no idea. In future, Jenny, I will try to see to it that our clothes are sewn in a reputable place. That at least I can do. In any event," she amended, thinking of her mother, "I can but try."

"And your friend—the poor creature with the child—was she a seamstress too?"

"Oh, no. I know little of her. She had a room in a lodging house near where I worked, and we was used to meet sometimes and talk. She's a poor deceived maid who comes from farming folk, like myself. Being righteous people they turned her out when her plight was discovered, but I couldn't find it in myself to condemn her. She loved the man too much. I pitied her, and she seemed to find comfort in talking to me.

"Then when I was destitute, she took me into her room, but indeed, she is in worse case than myself. She had been living on a sum that her baby's father gave her, but that has been finished some time now."

"And would he help her no more?"

"It seems not. She tried to see him, but was cruelly repulsed by servants. She never told me his name, only that he was a gentleman."

"That he was not," cried Georgina. "Would a true gentleman serve any woman so bitterly?"

"Some of them take their pleasures where they will and never heed the trouble they cause. He knew—his servants must have told him how bad a case the child and his mother were in, but it seemed he did not care. Then three days ago we were turned out of our room for owing rent."

"How abominably cruel!"

"It could have been worse. At least the landlady did not have us arrested for debt, as she could have done. She said it was on account of the baby and she having one the same age. We were in the park because a kind milkmaid took pity and helped us feed the baby, Queeney being so starved she had little sustenance left in her own body. Begging your pardon, miss, I should not talk so to you, a well-born lady. You can have no idea of such matters."

"You are wrong. I have not been always living in London dressed in fine clothes, Jenny, and one day I shall return to the country. I find my greatest fulfillment in helping the sick and needy.

"I require a maid. Could you fill that post, think you? Would you later consider living with me in straitened circumstances?"

"Oh, miss, I'd go anywhere, do anything for you. Can you really mean what you say?"

As Georgina smilingly assented, the girl continued eagerly, her thin cheeks bright pink now, her eyes shining. "I'll work my fingers to the bone for you, I promise. And I am cunning with my needle and can make all manner of trifles for you. Also, I was used to dress my mother's hair and several other women of the village and was many times complimented on my skill."

Georgina left Jenny dreaming joyfully of the future and descended the stairs to find her mother in a silk wrapper, languidly eating a breakfast of bread and butter and tea. She looked surprised to see her daughter. "You appear so fresh, my love, as if you had been out of doors this morning."

"Indeed I have, ma'am, and I have to tell you that we can no longer receive the Earl of Rivington. His behaviour has been abominable."

Mrs. Havard gave a faint scream. "What can you mean? Speak, for heaven's sake!"

Georgina described her walk and rescue by Lord Rivington and her mother cried, "What humiliation! Georgina, how could you allow yourself to be drawn into such a position? Why must you always be upsetting us so? And what, pray, can it signify whether or not we receive his lordship? Surely I owe him thanks, miss, and an apology too, for having a daughter who forces him to tangle with such vulgar people."

"Wait, Mama. When you have heard the rest you will be in no doubt of your future attitude towards this . . . this libertine."

Mrs. Havard's eyes grew round with horror. "What can he have done? Has he molested you?"

For a split second the memory of her first meeting with the Earl flashed into Georgina's brain. It served to add fire to her present denunciation. As quickly as possible she told of Queeney's reaction to Lord Rivington and Jenny's subsequent explanation. By now Mrs. Havard was very confused.

"Do you mean to tell me that you have brought a discarded female and her child into this house . . . that they are even now upstairs?"

"No, Mama," Georgina explained patiently, "Jenny is an innocent girl whom I have engaged to be my maid. I am sure Peregrine will not object when he hears her story. She has been so badly treated, mama, starved and overworked and now turned into the streets without any form of subsistence."

"But, my dear," protested Mrs. Havard feebly, "I know these things are terrible, but they happen all the time. One simply cannot always be . . ." At the sight of the anger in her daughter's face she wavered, "I am sure you are right, my love. If the girl is respectable, no doubt . . . But what has that to do with Rivington?"

"I have been trying to tell you, Mama. When the other woman showed him her baby—and it had a shock of black curls exactly like his own—he seemed to experience no surprise. He asked his friend, Mr. Briton, to take me away."

"Very proper of him," pronounced her mother.

"Then later he sent for his travelling coach to be sent to Hyde Park. Don't you see, Mama, he would not even take the risk of allowing her to be seen near his residence—he cannot wait to hide the poor deceived creature and his . . . his . . ."

"Georgina! I forbid you even to think such a word!"

"Baby," continued Georgina, "on his estates in Berkshire. He is aware that I know of his shocking conduct and cannot expect me to condone it. Now do you see why you must not admit him again."

"*Must* not!" declared Mrs. Havard. "Remember you speak to your mother." Then, again encountering her daughter's accusing gaze, she sank on to the sofa with closed eyes. "If only your father were here," she moaned. "If society were to cut all the young men who . . . who behaved with impropriety, there would be almost no one left. This kind of thing happens, my dear. I am sorry about the poor little baby, but we must accept that gentlemen have a licence in such matters. Now pray leave me—your exuberance—so early—my head—ring for Webster, please . . ."

Georgina turned hopelessly away. She might have known her protest would be useless. At least her mother had raised no serious objection to her taking Jenny for a maid. She was surprised when Eliza did not grumble at being released for kitchen duties until Jenny, having met the below stairs staff, confided that "it was no wonder Eliza didn't mind. It seems she's very taken with the chef."

"And does he return her affection?" asked Georgina, amused.

"Ah, that I can't say, him being French and me not understanding half what he says. Course, Eliza don't either, but that don't seem to bother her. I expect she'll get him in the end. Her sort generally have their way." She gave an expressive sniff before going out to buy stuff to make raiment suitable for the abigail of a young lady of quality.

Peregrine joined Georgina for luncheon, and she told him about Jenny. "I hope you do not mind my taking the girl on, Perry."

"Lord, no, what can one more signify in such a household

as this? Where are Mama and Penelope? Shopping again, I suppose."

She caught an inflection of bitterness and joined her brother at the window, where he stood staring at a passing coach.

"Look out there, George, different from Havard Hall ain't it? Do you think you will ever settle again when . . . when all this is past?"

He seemed not to listen to her assurances, but continued, "Mama tells me that you and Penelope are to be presented at the next Drawing Room. Is it true that a court dress can cost as much as three hundred guineas?"

"More, much more," cried Georgina, "if all I hear is correct, though ours will not do so. Miss Ingram's was nearer five hundred, and with her jewels, she represented more than your whole lottery money. She must have looked very beautiful."

"And very wealthy," sighed Peregrine.

"Do you really care for her?"

He flung away from the window and began to pace the floor. "I care! And what will it avail me? Nothing! I tell you, George, it was a bad day which brought us here."

"Why, what can you mean?"

He did not answer immediately, and she realised suddenly that his face bore tiny lines which certainly had not been there when they had come to town. He turned troubled eyes to her. "I've got to tell someone, love, though it isn't fair it should be you. What can you do?"

"Perry, for heaven's sake do not keep me in suspense. What has happened?"

He slumped into a chair dropping his head into his hands and his voice came muffled. "I've been such a fool. I should have listened when you suggested putting the money into the estate. Yet it seemed a fortune to me—a fortune."

"To me too," said Georgina. Her heart was pounding with anxiety, but she kept her voice even. "Tell me exactly what troubles you. You know I will always try to help."

"You can't. And when Penelope and Mama hear . . . The money seemed to melt away. This house, servants, carriages, horses, clothes, all have cost so much. The bills began to arrive soon after we got here. I wasn't worried at first. Lots of men about town only laugh at the duns, but I realise now that they are the ones with rich papas who can lift them out of their difficulties—and their creditors are indulgent and don't mind waiting till they reach their majority and control their own fortunes. It took everyone little time to recognise me for a poor man cutting his dash in town with nothing to back him."

"How . . . how bad is it?"

He raised his head and she was shocked to see his haggard looks. "As bad as may be. Oh, George, I simply cannot pay what I owe."

"Perry, don't look so. We must tell Penelope and Mama and return home at once. If we explain to your creditors that we will pay in time—why, the timber on the estate will fetch a good sum, and we can make the farms yield a profit if we work."

"You're a good sister, but it's useless. I once told you I did not care for games of chance played in a big way and nor do I, yet in a frantic effort to raise money I allowed myself to be drawn in. At first I won, then I began to lose. Instead of realising how green I am, I plunged deeper. Debts of honour must be paid—I should be branded for life if I failed in this—so I went to the money lenders. I was desperate. I tried to read all their bits of paper, but could not make sense of them, so I ended by simply signing anything they handed me in return for money. It seemed so easy. Now I find I am committed to paying back sums which will take all my life even if I *can* make the estates pay."

"Did you borrow so much?"

"Not such a large sum, but the rates are cruelly high. You would scarce credit how deep in I am."

He rose and touched her arm gently. "Forgive me, I should not trouble you this way. It is for me to take the bur: den of what I have done. I am no better than our father was. Perhaps for the first time, I begin to understand him."

"Did not Sir Francis Calland warn you?"

"Oh, yes, he has been the soul of amiability, but I was introduced into the most unscrupulous places by men whom now I think are employed to lure greenhorns like me."

"Perry, whatever happens we must return home at once. To stay here will only incur further expense."

"No, that is not the way. In any case, the house is paid for to the end of the term, and only allow the duns to catch a whiff of panic and they will be down on me. Something may happen . . ."

"The court dresses must be cancelled before it is too late," declared Georgina. "I do not care a fig for being presented, and I am sure that when Penelope hears . . ."

"I care!" Her brother's vehemence made her start. "I tell you, I love Charlotte Ingram, and how will she look upon me if I cancel such a public arrangement? And if you think that Penelope will meekly accept the idea of losing her presentation you must see her through a rosy haze. She and Mama are full of the offer they expect from Sir Stannard Morton. He is rich enough to afford Penelope and not mind her lack of fortune—but let a scandal break over our heads, and he will bolt like a terrified rabbit.

"And don't begin to remind me of her other adorers. It is simply the fashion to worship at the shrine of the latest beauty. If we do not keep up appearances, she will lose her chance of a fine marriage and be immured at Havard Hall until she finds some red-faced squire to take her.

"Imagine having to live with her lamentations, George. A debtors' gaol would be better by far."

She shuddered. "Don't, Perry, not even in fun. It could not come to that. It could not, could it?"

"I tell you I don't know . . . I don't know . . ."

He flung out of the room, and in a moment she heard the slam of the front door. Before she could collect her thoughts, the butler announced, "Mr. Anthony Briton, miss."

Lord Rivington's friend bowed and accepted Georgina's invitation to seat himself, but refused refreshment. "We are scarcely acquainted, Miss Havard, but I felt I must call. I wished to assure myself that you were quite safe after your distressing experience."

She flushed slightly beneath his open gaze. "My distressing experience, as you call it, was nothing compared with that of the poor girl we met. I think it a most shameful occurrence when a gentleman of wealth and standing can so ill use a woman."

"I'm sure you are wrong, ma'am. I know that Lord Rivington will have an explanation which absolves him. He is gone out of town, but I have received a message saying that he will return tomorrow."

"He is no doubt settling the young woman and his . . . her child where they will cause him no further embarrassment."

Mr. Briton's voice grew cool. "I have been friends with the Earl these many years, in fact, I was his only boyhood friend, and I have never known him deliberately to hurt a woman."

"It seems to be common knowledge that he takes what pleasures in life he desires. I speak more plainly than you are perhaps accustomed to hear from a woman, but I am not one of your niminy-piminy misses. I care for my sisters, whatever their station."

"He is no worse and a good deal better than many men of fashion," burst out Mr. Briton. Then he paused and spoke more moderately, "Miss Havard, his lordship spoke to me of you . . ."

"That I do not doubt, sir. He could not miss an opportunity to amuse himself and others at my expense."

Except for a frown that crossed his face he continued as if

she had not spoken . . ."and I know you to be a lady who cares for others and who expresses herself quite . . . quite forcibly on occasion. Believe me, I have only admiration for you."

His smile was gentle, and the sympathy in his warm brown eyes almost brought the tears which had been threatening for hours. She gasped, "Lord Rivington despises me . . . not that you are to think I care a jot for his opinion."

"Of course not, ma'am," he agreed.

There was a brief silence before he spoke again, hesitantly, "My friend does not seek pity from anyone, but although you do not care for his views about yourself, I have an impression that he is concerned for yours about him. It may help you to understand why he appears to be so harsh if I reveal something of his background. I must trust you not to tell him I have done so, as he would be excessively angry with me."

The impulse to deny any interest in Alexander Rivington died at birth. She despised herself for her curiosity, but it was too strong to be smothered, and she urged him on.

"Lord Rivington's father was an extremely cold man. Alexander and his three sisters were subjected to harsher treatment than any given to the poorest child on the estates. He said he believed that a strict regime was necessary for children of high birth to enable them to live as strong, proud aristocrats. Yet it is my private belief that he was cruel to his son and daughters because he was a mean man.

"He forced them to bath all year round in icy water; only let them show a dislike of any food and it would be served at every meal; he himself whipped them mercilessly if they deviated in any way from the path he made them tread. I have seen weals on Alexander which made me sick."

"What of their mother?" asked Georgina in a low voice.

"She, poor lady, was as subject as they—perhaps more so. She took a fortune to her husband, but he allowed her only a pittance. He cared nothing for her comfort."

"Such is the lot of women in these so-called civilised times!"

"I don't wonder at your bitterness, but I have not told you the worst. The children were all taken ill of a fever. In spite of their mother's entreaties the harshness continued—including the cold bathing until . . . until . . ."

"Yes," prompted Georgina gently.

"The three little girls died."

"Oh, no! How could he?"

"Alexander recovered. Thank God he was exceptionally strong, but it will be no surprise to you to learn that he and his mother never forgave his father."

"Where is Lady Rivington now? Does Lord Rivington care for her?"

"He adores her. As soon as he left home for Oxford University she ran away. Friends sheltered her until Alexander was able to make a humble home for her in Oxford. Somehow they kept her residence a secret from her husband, chiefly because Alexander gave her an allowance from the miserable sum he himself was given. I was at Oxford at the same time, and I know the privations he cheerfully endured for his mother's sake.

"When he was two and twenty, his father died and he inherited vast entailed wealth and estates. His first task was to settle his mother into a comfortable home; next he attended to the sorry state of many of his tenants. Lord Rivington is not quite what the world believes."

Georgina had a vision of a small boy, grey eyes anguished as he suffered; tear-filled, as he saw the deaths of his sisters. Her heart softened. Then the images were overlaid by that of a starving baby with a shock of black hair so like his lordship's own.

"I regret that his past miseries do not seem to have made him compassionate, Mr. Briton. Who can tell what other perfidies lie hidden?"

He flinched, and she felt sorry for him. It was evident that he loved his friend. "He is fortunate indeed to have so loyal a supporter as yourself, sir. I will try, if I can, to see him through your eyes."

Scarcely had he left when the butler announced Sir Francis Calland. He entered, dressed as always, with fashionable elegance.

"Miss Havard, how pleasant to see you. I asked for Peregrine, but discovered you were the only member of the family at home. Was not that Anthony Briton I saw leaving?"

As Georgina confirmed this, he continued, "I thought I was not mistaken, though we move in different circles, of course. I believe he is a great admirer of Rivington's. I daresay he has been trying to excuse the events of the morning."

"How do you know?" gasped Georgina.

"All the world knows and is laughing. One would expect so experienced a man of the town as my noble cousin to conduct his little affairs with more skill than to have them exposed in a public park. The scene was witnessed with relish by nurse girls and grooms—and servants talk, I fear."

Georgina raised her brows. "Servants' gossip, Sir Francis."

His smile did not touch his light eyes. "Alas, one cannot do without it if one is to keep in touch with events, regrettable though it may seem. It is known that you left the park with commendable haste, and missed much of the degradation. It is to your credit. I daresay none of us will ever know the full ugly story."

She flushed, realising it was impossible to continue with any further denial and tried to change the subject. "Mr. Briton was talking of Lord Rivington's hard upbringing. As his cousin, you are no doubt aware of the facts—those poor little children . . ."

"Oh, has he been on that tack again? Poor Anthony Briton. I suppose one must admire his loyalty, but you must know, Miss Havard, that he is but the son of the Head Steward of the Rivington estates. His father was well born, but the youngest of a poor family and was employed by the old Earl at a mean salary, the greatest part of his payment being that Anthony should be educated as befitted the son of a gentleman. His mother died at his birth and much of his boyhood was spent in the Rivington nurseries. I believe the girls received no education save that which their mama was able to give them."

He smiled again at Georgina with more warmth. "Must we continue to discuss such tedious matters? There are more interesting subjects a man may talk of with a woman."

She felt flustered. Was he amusing himself at her expense? He must know she was without fortune or prospects.

Quickly she said, "It is true, is it not, that Lord Rivington cares deeply for his mother?"

Sir Francis sighed. "I see our Mr. Briton has been trotting out his hobbyhorses. Well, then, let us continue to talk of his noble lordship and exhaust the topic once for all.

"The truth here is that the Countess put herself beyond the respect of society when she ran away from her husband's rightful dominion. She was forced to live as best she could, and once it was even rumoured that she hired herself as a cook-maid, but I doubt she sank so low."

"There is nothing degrading in honest toil," flashed Georgina. "What is a woman to do if she is mistreated by one who must, under our laws, be her natural protector?"

"*If* she was so mistreated. One has only the word of Rivington and the so faithful Mr. Briton for that, and my noble cousin has always been close-mouthed about the whole affair."

"Then did not the three small girls die of a neglected fever?"

"A fever? Yes! Many children do so die, do they not? Neglected? Who can tell?"

As she opened her mouth to speak again he flung up an arm as if to deflect a rapier thrust. "Do not direct your darts this way, I implore. I am all sympathy for your indignation, but the truth is that Rivington is ashamed of his mother and has sequestered her in a corner of one of his estates—by no means his largest.

"The good lady, I collect, is living a life of humble poverty, taking on many household tasks far below her rank and even labouring in the garden for food. Do not be taken in by Mr. Briton, who owes his present government appointment to the patronage of Lord Rivington, and is naturally anxious to show the world he cares for his patron."

When Georgina would have questioned him further he skillfully turned the conversation to the previous night's play and shortly after took his departure, bowing so low over her hand she believed he might kiss it.

She was surprised by an impulse to jerk her hand away, and a strong sense of relief when his lips only hovered for a moment before he rose. Long after he had gone she sat thinking, wondering whom to believe, and trying to resolve the tableaux which kept unfolding in her mind; of a small boy, his trusting grey eyes grown hard and suspicious with the endurance of his own sufferings and those of his loved ones; of a young woman desperate with the anguish of abandonment and starvation of herself and her child; of her brother sick with anxieties which she now shared.

She pictured Peregrine lying in the filth and degradation of a debtors' gaol, hopeless in the knowledge that there would be no money to relieve his sufferings.

She had reached the point at which the terrible gaol fever had taken her brother's life when her head began to ache, and she retired to her room for the rest of the day, cancelling her attendance at a card party with her mother and Penelope, and insisting that she felt too ill even to talk to them.

She felt ashamed of her unsociability, but felt quite unequal to witnessing their happiness at their present life, knowing as she did, that everything could soon disintegrate around them.

CHAPTER 7

Next day at breakfast Mrs. Havard was full of complaints. "Penelope's bonnet does not suit her and will have to be given away and another purchased. The milliner was so persuasive that I had not time to think. And when I compared the pink ribbons which we bought to make more love knots on your sister's gown I find they do not match at all.

"It is too provoking as I shall now be forced to spend my day searching for the right shade—Penelope desires to wear her new gown tonight at Lady Sarah's musical evening and Sir Stannard is to be there—he expressed a particular liking for pink ribbons. I have such high hopes of him . . ."

Georgina stopped the flow of words. "Where is Penelope, Mama?"

"She is resting. I told her, 'My love,' I said, 'you must rest whenever possible to preserve your complexion. Gentlemen like a girl to be in looks and not show signs of the night's gaiety, though they would soon remark if she were not present on every fashionable occasion.'

"And last night's *soirée* lasted so far into dawn and I was never more bored. Only dancing for the young ones and indifferent entertainment for the rest of us, and I declare, I would be ashamed to serve such meagre food. Still, if one is a Duchess one can afford not to mind what people say, I suppose . . ."

"If you are fatigued, Mama, I will try to match the ribbons for you."

"Oh, would you? What a dear girl you can be at times. But you will be absolutely sure to obtain an exact shade, will you not? You must take them right out to the street into full daylight, you know.

"Since you love to walk, you will not require the carriage. I particularly wish to take Penelope driving in Hyde Park today. Sir Stannard told me most significantly that he was used to drive there most mornings."

At mid-day Georgina left the house and walked to Bond Street, accompanied by Jenny. The day was bright, but as yet the sun gave little warmth, and a chill April breeze tugged her skirts. She was glad to keep up a brisk pace and snuggle her hands into her large fur muff.

She was fortunate in being able to match the ribbons easily and turned toward home, strolling slower now, hoping that by the time she returned her mother and sister would have left for their drive. She decided to give the ribbons to Webster and go with Jenny for a walk in Green Park.

The sound of trotting horses and carriage wheels was too common to cause her to look round until she was addressed by a voice she knew well.

"Good morning, Miss Havard."

She turned sharply to see Lord Rivington, seated in his curricle, holding in check a pair of spirited match greys. She watched with appreciation, those strong hands encased in gauntlets, as they handled the reins gently but firmly, so that the horses became quieter, stamping mildly and blowing through their noses.

The Earl was able now to give her his full attention. As she caught the bold look in his grey eyes she felt suddenly glad to be wearing her new brown velvet pelisse and bonnet with the curling yellow plumes. At the same instant she realised that she had been standing for several seconds apparently waiting for him to speak and she coloured.

"I had not expected you in London this morning, sir," she snapped, confusion sharpening her voice.

The Earl's brows rose, "No, madam?"

She became aware that she had opened the conversation in a style which she regretted, and unable to think of a graceful way to continue, she turned away. "I am sure you have much to do, my lord."

"Not anything which will not await your pleasure." Then, ordering his groom to take the reins, he leapt lightly down and stood blocking her path.

She clenched her hands inside her muff. "I cannot pass, Lord Rivington."

"Please do me the honour of taking a short drive with me," he answered, giving her a small bow.

She wanted to refuse. She ached to be able to hurl her refusal in his arrogant face, but she sensed, rather than saw, the eyes of the servants upon her. The approach of a group of chattering, laughing ladies and gentlemen decided her. She withdrew a hand from her muff and held it out to him, "A short drive then," she said coldly, "no more."

He handed her into the curricle, gave a quick order to his groom, and before she gathered exactly what was happening, she was being driven away at a spanking pace, leaving the groom and Jenny behind.

"What means this, sir? I do not wish to proceed without my maid."

"You will be perfectly safe with me, I assure you."

She bit her lip to stop a retort which could lead only to further humiliation and fixed her eyes ahead, only realising, as the horses were gentled through gates, that they were entering Hyde Park.

Here she was forced to bow and smile at several acquaintances who drove, rode or walked in the sun, and even in her annoyance could not fail to notice the envious looks of some of the girls who stared to see her in the Earl's curricle. His lordship was not known to elevate many young ladies to such an exalted place.

Presently the horses were pulled to a walk, and the Earl looked into her face. "I did not answer your first remark, I recall. I rose at dawn and drove fast to be here this morning. I have a particular call I must make."

"I spoke without thought. It is of no concern to me what you do."

"Is it not? I understood from Briton whom I met earlier

that you felt very strongly about certain aspects of my life."
He smiled. "I believe the good fellow made an attempt to
justify my character to you. He confessed, with a good deal
of embarrassment, that he had so far forgotten himself as to
relate some incidents from my past."

"I was not prying!"

"I would never accuse you of vulgar curiosity, Miss Havard. But in any case, you are welcome to know as much of
me as will interest you."

Was there no way she could set him down? Had he no
shame? While she searched her mind for a way to change the
course of their talk, he said, "That girl who attended you—is
she not the other of the pair we met in the park?"

Georgina could only trust herself to nod.

"I thought so. Poor creature, she is so thin, though now
much better clad. Your doing, I daresay."

"I have taken her for my maid."

"I see. In my preoccupation yesterday I forgot her for a
while, then when I searched for her she was gone. I showed
her a lack of consideration which I am happy you rectified.
Queeney told me what a good girl she is."

Georgina's face flamed. "Showed her lack of consideration," she repeated. "And if that is what you call your
treatment of her, by what name does your other conduct go
by?"

She could have cut out her tongue as soon as the words
were out. She dreaded his next speech, but he only said mildly, "I should have guessed that you would look after the girl.
I daresay she has had no training in attending a lady of quality, but then, I collect that you do not care for such—er—
flummery."

It was a deliberate reference to Georgina's conduct on
their second meeting, and she almost ground her teeth. "Be
so good, sir, as to take me home."

"As you wish, ma'am," he said and something in his voice
gave her a curious feeling that in some way she had disappointed him.

As they bowled towards the exit she caught sight of two stationary carriages, one containing the gorgeously apparelled figure of Sir Stannard, the other her mother and Penelope, agape to see where she was.

She had a terrible desire to giggle and glanced sideways at her companion. Had a corner of his mouth twitched? She could not think so. He looked perfectly solemn.

They remained silent until they reached the house in Upper Brook Street, when the Earl asked, "Can you descend without assistance? I fear my horses are still too fresh to leave unattended."

"I can manage perfectly well, thank you," she retorted and leapt down with reckless speed. The hem of her gown caught in her half-boot and the delicate muslin ripped audibly.

Catching up her drooping hem in her hand, she ran up the steps and tapped her foot furiously as she waited to be admitted. Then she fled to her bed-chamber to be greeted by a tutting Jenny, who went straight to her workbasket for needle and cotton. Georgina scarcely heard her maid's enquiries as to how the accident happened. She was sure that just before the curricle was driven away she had heard a low laugh.

As Jenny sewed she paced up and down, her fists clenching and unclenching as she felt a very unladylike desire to punch his noble lordship, the Earl of Rivington, on the nose. How dare he force her to drive with him? How dare he have the audacity to mock her and laugh at her? She would be thankful when the Season ended and she could return to the peace of the countryside.

This thought drew her mind abruptly to her brother and his disclosures. Perhaps they would all find themselves at Havard Hall sooner than they expected. And she felt her heart sink unaccountably at the idea. For some unfathomable reason the quiet life she had always lived no longer beckoned as it should.

And she felt a sharp pang of pity for her mother. It looked

as if history would repeat itself, and she would again be pushed out of the society she loved into a life she detested. And this time she would suffer even more if Penelope lost her chance of an advantageous marriage.

She went to the wash-stand and splashed her face with cold water, then held out her arms for Jenny to help her into her gown, now so skilfully mended that one would be hard put to find the stitches. She passively allowed the girl to comb and dress her hair, but they did not speak. Between them a great friendship and understanding was growing, and Georgina felt Jenny's silent sympathy, though the maid could not guess the reason for her agitation.

As she entered the drawing room she heard a strong rapping at the front door and the murmur of voices. Callers! Well, she would instruct the butler to say she was not at home. But when he appeared and announced in solemn tones: "The Earl of Rivington, miss," she was struck dumb with surprise long enough for the servant to withdraw and show his lordship into her presence.

She sat on the edge of a small satin-covered chair and tried to control the pounding of her heart. Was she never to have any peace from him? He entered, and with a strong effort, she raised her eyes to meet his calmly.

She did not offer her hand and he gave a small bow, murmuring, "Your servant, ma'am." He looked grave and his face was expressionless except for a gleam which appeared in his eyes as he glanced down towards the hem of her dress.

She waved her hand at a sofa as far removed from herself as possible and said faintly, "Please be seated, sir. I will ring for refreshment. I regret the absence of my mother and sister."

"As I do not, thank you. If I had not known them to be at this moment in Hyde Park, enjoying the company of your sister's conquest, I should not have called."

"Oh! But they could by now have returned."

"Not so. I have but moments ago sent a fellow to check on their movements."

At this evidence of his audacity she fell silent long enough for him to pick up a small chair, place it in front of her and seat himself upon it, saying, "I desire only to talk with you."

"But we have parted not an hour since. Anything you have to say to me could have been communicated then."

"I do not agree. I wish to speak to you in an atmosphere of privacy and tranquillity."

The latter emotion was far from Georgina's mind as he sat for a while in silence. Her brain seethed in an effort to find some topic of conversation which would not lead her into yet another pit of embarrassment. Her efforts were unrewarded, and she sat as still as the Earl, her hands in her lap, refusing to meet his gaze. When he did begin to speak, she found difficulty at first in comprehending the meaning of his words.

". . . regret sincerely that our relationship should have developed into one of misunderstandings and annoyances. I have given much thought to what I am about to say, Miss Havard. It is this: I would offer you the protection of my name."

She looked dazedly at him. "The . . . the protection of your name?"

"That is so. You have not misheard my words."

Now she lifted her pale face to his, and her eyes glowed green. "How dare you," she breathed. "I suppose you would use me as you did that other poor creature."

For an instant he looked astonished, then he smiled, a wolfish grin which made her shudder. "Ah, yes, the woman in the park. Forgive me, my dear Miss Havard, I had forgot."

"Forgot! Oh, men like you make me bitterly angry. That girl was decent once, and now she is ruined. How many more have you . . . ?"

"Very few, I assure you, madam. And as it happens I was not proposing your seduction and a place as my mistress. I was, and am, offering you my hand in marriage."

The words fell between them into Georgina's appalled

silence. Then she found her voice. "Marriage! To you!"

"The idea shocks you? I can promise you that many women would find such a proposal flattering in the extreme."

"Your conceit does you no credit. And I am not one of those women."

"You make that abundantly clear—and it is not conceit which inspires that remark, but honesty on which I think you pride yourself. But that is not the point in question. Consider a moment before you persist in a refusal. You would have an unassailable position in society. I am a very rich man and could help your whole family—including using my power to clear your brother's debts."

At her quick look of alarm he smiled. "Oh, I know of them. Master Peregrine is in deep with the money-lenders, and the knowledge could soon be all over town. What chance then will your mother and pretty little sister have of netting Sir Stannard?"

Georgina's pale skin flushed, then became paler still. His jibe at her family hurt, but there was truth in it, and her innate integrity forced her silence.

The Earl's voice became smoother. "Your mama would be delighted for you, and only think, I have estates full of ignorant people who suffer from a wide variety of diseases. I would not interfere at all with your medical propensities so long as you kept clear of infection, your activities within the bounds of propriety, and did not neglect your duties as my wife and mistress of many large establishments."

Georgina's cheeks were now paper white. Every word he spoke seemed calculated to wound, and this condescending reference to her longings to be a physician thrust deep into her tenderest feelings.

For once she could not defend herself. The hurt was too great and she would not lay herself open to another attack. All she could stammer was, "You have not, I collect, approached my mother or my brother. This is yet another insult you place upon me. If you were in earnest . . ."

"Why, Miss Havard, you astonish me. What means this? I took you for a woman of independent spirit. Indeed, you have been at pains to make this clear. If, however, you prefer me to consult with your guardians before I have your answer . . . ?"

His eyes held mockery in their grey depths and Georgina felt that no words could be too frank to depress the pretensions of a man who so tormented her.

She said in a low voice, "Even had I supposed you serious, I could not bring myself to accept a man in whom all honour seems lost. If you marry anyone, let it be the mother of your base-born child—an innocent who will suffer all its life."

The Earl rose to his feet and stared down at her. He seemed about to speak, then checked himself and studied her. His expression unfathomable, he said softly, "What is this? You hold yourself to be an emancipated woman. Your heroine, Mary Wollstonecraft, herself, did not hesitate to live as a man's wife, yes, and to bear him a child. Surely if she condones such behaviour, it is not fitting for you to condemn."

Georgina's breast rose and fell in frustrated rage. "It is not the same—she chose her path."

"And did not the young woman of whom we speak choose hers?"

"You, sir, are the best judge of that."

"To be sure—my memory will keep playing me false."

Georgina sprang to her feet and walked swiftly to the door. She must bring this terrible interview to an end. "You do not wish to marry me, Lord Rivington. You do not care for me."

He was close to her before she could escape, and his hands gripped her arms with bruising strength. "You are wrong, Miss Georgina Havard. I want you. For me you have attractions which other women lack. You infuriate me, but you intrigue me. You anger but amuse me. In short, you never bore me. Oh, if you could but know what that means to me. I am told repeatedly that it is my duty to marry and it has been borne in upon me that I could endure to live with you. That it would, in fact, be pleasing to me."

She shivered in her cold fury. So she was to marry him to amuse him, was she? She would be his plaything, his toy, the mother of his necessary heirs, conceived and borne in a loveless marriage because the great Lord Rivington did not find her a bore.

"Marry me, Georgina," he murmured, "marry me soon."

She began to struggle, but her efforts to free herself were unavailing. She stopped and looked straight into his eyes. "I will not marry you, sir. I hate you, and worse, I despise you. I abominate you for what you are and for the cruelty and oppression which you represent. When—if—I marry, it will not be such a one as you."

The Earl's face darkened beneath the contemptuous lash of her tongue, and his grip tightened. Georgina cried out. "You are hurting me."

"Good," he grated. "I would like to hurt you more. You have said unforgivable things to me."

He moved with catlike speed and she found herself imprisoned within the circle of one arm while with his free hand he forced her chin up and her head back. As once before, his saturnine face came closer to hers until his breath was warm on her mouth. He paused and she tried to speak, but no words came, and she realised with horror that she wanted him to kiss her.

Rake, libertine, man of no principles he was, but with all her mind and body she longed for his lips on hers. She glanced quickly into his eyes before she closed her lids, but that look was enough to tell her that he recognised her innermost feelings.

His lips came down on hers with passionate hunger, and she felt herself responding. Without volition, without control to stem the rising tide of her own need she returned kiss for kiss until he thrust her from him and stood panting.

"What are you?" he rasped. "You offer me hatred and contempt, yet your kisses tell a different story. This is something new to me."

Shame flooded her. "Leave me, for God's sake," she begged. "You are wicked . . . you make me . . ."

He reached out for her again. "Georgina . . ."

But she eluded him and ran across the room. With a muffled oath he followed, stumbled over a small stool, and almost lost his balance. She had time to wrench open the door and escape to her room to throw herself with a strangled cry on the bed.

"I hate him—hate him!" she sobbed into her pillow, but even as her lips formed the words, her heart told her otherwise. She could not help herself. She loved Alexander Rivington no matter what he was, but she could not marry him, and she had rejected him in a manner which must have left him with the impression that she was a wanton with principles which stemmed only from her tongue. No woman who was not a shameless coquette could have kissed him as she had just done, especially after protesting her loathing for him.

Hearing a soft scratch at the door, she sat up. "Who is it?"

"Only me, miss." Jenny's voice was sharp with alarm and Georgina bade her enter. Her maid looked at her with concern.

"Oh, madam, it's not my place to speak, I know, but you are so unhappy today. If there's aught I can do . . ."

Georgina managed a smile. "You could bring me my harts horn—if I had any. I vow I'm beginning to suffer as much from the vapours as any lady of fashion."

"Not you, miss," the maid maintained stoutly. "If you weep, then I don't doubt 'tis for something worth your tears."

Georgina turned away. Jenny's gentle soul would be

shocked if she knew the truth. The maid came to her now with a cloth wrung out in lavender water and insisted that her mistress relax on the bed. Georgina was so unused to such tender treatment that it almost brought fresh tears, but she surrendered herself to the kind ministrations and lay still, the sweet-scented cloth cool on her forehead. Her heart began to resume its normal beat, and she was able to give Jenny a much warmer smile.

"I little knew what a treasure I had found that day in the park, Jenny. I'm thankful I was passing at the right moment."

"Oh, so am I, Miss Georgina," answered Jenny fervently, "and so is Queeney. The Earl of Rivington gave me a message from her before he left just now: she is well and she and the babe are thriving on good country air and food. Wasn't it kind of him to think of such a thing, and he so far above me."

"I am delighted to hear of Queeney's good fortune," murmured Georgina, but inwardly she seethed. What kind of a man was he, this great Earl? He could seduce an innocent girl and abandon her; then when his treachery was discovered, hide her in the country away from the world. Yet he could think of the anxiety of a friend and remember to obtain news to ease her worry.

He seemed swayed by any wind which blew, and Georgina felt a fresh surge of emotion in which contempt and desire warred to gain mastery in her.

Her turbulent feelings made her speak more sharply than she intended as she said, "I wonder at your seeing Lord Rivington in so kind a light after the way he has treated your friend."

Jenny shrugged. "As to that, miss, there is many a girl brought to her ruin by the likes of his lordship, yet few would engage to protect her as he has done now. He has atoned for his earlier neglect."

Georgina bit back bitter words. How could Jenny understand her resentment of a world where a woman must always show gratitude to a man for his attentions however grudgingly given? His child might have died of starvation had not chance brought it to the Earl's notice.

Her bed-chamber door was suddenly thrust open, and Mrs. Havard hurried into the room. "Leave us, girl," she commanded Jenny, and Georgina swung her legs to the floor as she saw the agitation of her mother.

"Mama, pray sit down, here in the chair near the fire. It is the most comfortable."

Mrs. Havard shook her head and her ruby eardrops swung and flashed. "I cannot sit—I cannot be still. Oh, Georgina, I have heard such a rumour. What will become of us if it should be founded in truth?"

Georgina feared she was beginning to understand, but she asked gently, "What rumour, Mama?"

"Have you then not heard? Perhaps it is only a wicked lie put about to torment me. People can be so cruel—society rends those who offend. I should know—your father made enemies . . ." She took a turn about the room, watched by her anxious daughter. "Penelope and I went to call on Lady Sarah, and the Duchess of Stockley was there. I tell you, I was paying her little attention—duchess she may be, but she is a tedious person, and mean with her entertainment as I've had occasion to mention . . .

"Well, that's as may be—I suppose one in so exalted a position may flout the conventions if she chooses, but then I heard her mention my son's name."

Georgina felt quick alarm which she hid from her mother.

"She had the audacity to say that he took well after his father."

"But, surely, Mama . . ."

"No, it was not what she said, but her manner of speaking! She intended her words to sound insulting, and I did not miss the inflection. Naturally I tried to discover her meaning, but she laughed and said that I would know all too soon that Peregrine could equal his father in games of chance—that the town was talking, but that she supposed all boys must have their fling.

"Then she said, almost under her breath, but so that I could hear, you apprehend, that it was well for young men to live high—provided they could pay the reckoning. I tell you, Georgina, it sent a shiver down my back. I expected someone to turn the matter to a jest, but one glance at the others frightened me. Where is Peregrine? I knew he played—what young man does not—but nothing more than that."

Georgina tried to keep the fear out of her face, but distress had made her mother sharp, and she said abruptly, "You have heard something. Out with it. If you know anything it is your duty to tell me. You and Peregrine have always been close. It is to you he would turn if he needed a confidante."

"You are right, Mama, Peregrine has spoken to me. It seems he has been led astray by those quick to seize upon a boy's inexperience."

As gently as possible she told her mother what Peregrine had said and finished, "My brother hopes to find a means to free us from our difficulties."

"What means? He knows no one of substance who would assist us, and your father exhausted the patience of all our friends. Oh, God, I could not bear shame and disgrace again. Oh, the reckless, stupid boy. How could he?"

Georgina's pang of pity for her mother was tinged with anger on her brother's behalf. All his actions, however mistaken, had been directed toward helping his family, and she pointed this out. Mrs. Havard brushed her protestations aside and sank into a chair near the window. For a few moments the only sounds were her quick breathing and the tap-tapping of her nails on the sill. "Well," she said, finally, "I have kept creditors at bay before. I must try to do so again. Penelope must have her chance—she must!"

She glared at her eldest daughter. "And if you would

make some effort . . . If only you were . . ." She did not need to finish for Georgina to know her meaning. She was the first-born, the one who should marry first if only she had been lovely or clever enough to attract a rich suitor.

Georgina wondered for a moment what her mother would say if she knew that a short time ago she had rejected an offer from one of the richest and most powerful men in the kingdom. Well, that was something Mama never would discover. Suddenly she felt consumed by guilt. She might possess an independent spirit, but she had been told so often that it was the duty of a woman to marry to oblige her family that the doctrine must have taken root. She had had it in her reach to smooth the path of those she loved and selfishly she had destroyed her opportunity.

Perhaps it was not too late. Looking at her mother's ravaged face, she wondered whether, if she encouraged Lord Rivington, intimated that she would take him, he might disregard the recent scene and offer for her again.

Then she remembered his arrogance, his cruelty, the way he had taken her acceptance for granted when he proposed marriage, and her resolve hardened. Rather than be beholden to him, she would strive for the rest of her life to pay off their debts.

In their agitation Georgina and Mrs. Havard had scarcely been aware of some bustle taking place in the street below, followed by the distant ringing of the doorbell.

Then came the sound of swiftly approaching footsteps and a cry of, "Mama, where are you?" which made them stare at one another.

"It is Penelope," said Mrs. Havard, "and in great impatience. What can have happened?"

She half rose to her feet, then sank back into the chair as her beautiful daughter burst without ceremony into the room. "Georgina, have you seen . . . ? Oh, Mama, there you are. There is a most extraordinary person who has seated herself in the downstairs drawing room and says she has come to stay. She demands to see you, Mama, and says she is not accustomed to be kept waiting."

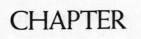

CHAPTER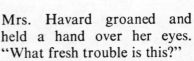

Mrs. Havard groaned and held a hand over her eyes. "What fresh trouble is this?"

Georgina's first thought had been that some creditor of Peregrine's had come to dun them, but she immediately rejected this as improbable. His duns were unlikely to be women. Her hand flew to her mouth as the idea struck her that perhaps her brother had added other, and perhaps infinitely more embarrassing, indiscretions to his folly.

"Penelope," she said urgently, "is this woman young? Is she pretty? How does she appear to you?"

Penelope sat down abruptly on the bed and giggled breathlessly. "How does she appear? Young? Pretty? Oh, no, not at all. Such a guy she is. If I had not been so afeared of her, I must have laughed in her face.

"She is wearing side panniers, on my honour, and a dress of bright green-and-pink-striped taffeta with enough stuff in it to make gowns for all three of us, supposing we would wear anything so hideous. And on her head there is a most odd contrivance of muslin framed on wire hoops, and I vow I caught a glimpse of very red hair, though a woman so old must surely be grey. I think it must be a wig.

"Who can she be, Mama? She spoke as if she knew you."

Mrs. Havard rose to her feet. "It is evident to me that I am to be plagued with yet another worry, as if I had not enough."

She walked from the room, sighing heavily, and the sisters stared at one another. Then they tiptoed to the half landing below, where they could hear the low murmur of their mother's voice from the drawing room and the strident tones of the stranger. The voices became raised, but the girls still could not catch words through the thickness of the door. Then, in response to a summons, the butler disappeared through the drawing room door and almost at once emerged and began to ascend the stairs.

With slightly raised brows he informed the young ladies that their mother required their immediate attendance.

Penelope had not exaggerated her description of the caller. She was a stout woman whose size was substantially increased by her gown, in a fashion of a former age, and by her high-crowned cap.

Then Georgina's amazed eyes were caught and held by a gaze from eyes set deep in a mass of wrinkles and whose unblinking stare held the potential ruthlessness of a sparrow hawk.

Mrs. Havard's voice was faint. "Make your curtseys, girls, to Lady Dorothea Lutterworth, the Dowager Countess of Fincham and a distant cousin of your dear Papa's."

As the girls rose the old countess snorted. "Dear Papa, indeed. Well, it's like you, Marianne, to forget your husband's faults, though from all I heard, you did not recognise them even when he was alive."

Mrs. Havard went pink. "My husband is dead. It is not seemly . . ."

She was interrupted. "Do not presume to criticise me, madam. I knew you when you were in your cradle. And if Havard had shown the least thought for his family, I would not have been driven to undertake a journey which has kept me on the road for seven days and in conditions of cold and damp such as a person of my years should not suffer."

Mrs. Havard spoke to her daughters. "Is it not good of Lady Dorothea? She has come to spend some time with us. I know we shall be glad of her company."

"Fiddlesticks! If I had not been informed that you were

all about to be disgraced in the eyes of polite society, I should not . . ."

Penelope gave a scream. "Disgraced? What does she mean, Mama? How disgraced?"

"Do you mean that your girls do not know of their brother's indiscretions?" demanded Lady Dorothea in aggressive tones.

"Georgina does," fluttered Mrs. Havard, "but I have tried to spare dear Penelope. She has such a tender constitution— so like my own."

"Nonsense!" stated Lady Dorothea. "You have the constitution of a work-horse—always had—although I know you find it convenient to slide out of difficult situations by pretending otherwise. And you, Miss Penelope, can stop working yourself into hysterics. Your brother has brought you to the brink of ruin, but I am here to save you. You will receive your proposal from Sir Stannard Morton, though if he is as spineless as his father and grandfather, I wish you joy of him."

Ignoring Penelope's pout, she turned to Georgina who started at finding herself suddenly the centre of attention. "So you are Georgina. My informant gave me to understand you possessed a certain quality of charm and beauty." Her tone made it clear she disagreed. "I *would* say, however, that you could be helped to distinction if only your hair were cut to suit your face and you stopped dressing in those missish, wishywashy clothes. In future I shall take it upon myself to attend your needs."

"I assure you, ma'am . . ." began Georgina.

Her words were halted by an imperious hand. "You will obey me, young lady. I am not accustomed to arguments from chits of your age."

Further protest was cut short as she tempered her words with a smile which riveted the attention of the Havard ladies. Her mouth was a wonder of gleaming, porcelain teeth which looked immeasurably incongruous in that wrinkled old face.

Then the teeth were abruptly covered as she asked Mrs. Havard to which of the local stables she should direct her coachman. "I have travelled with my barouche-and-four and a post chaise for my maid and footman. Then there is my bed linen to be unpacked as well as my chests of clothes. At inns I always use my own sheets, though I was agreeably surprised by some of the improvements which have been effected since my younger days. The inns are quite tolerable for the most part, though at one I was served with very indifferent green goose. I lay last night in the George at Uxbridge and was as comfortable as one may be from home . . ."

During this speech she had risen from the sofa, whose width was needed to accommodate her wide skirts, and walked majestically from the room, followed by a twittering Mrs. Havard.

Penelope sat down heavily. "She will be the ruin of us in society. How can one go out with such a person? All London will be laughing. And what does she mean about Peregrine? And how can she have known of our affairs? If she has been seven days on the road, she must live at the back of beyond."

Georgina explained as kindly as possible what trouble they were in. Her sister went white. "If he has ruined my chances of an advantageous marriage I will never forgive him."

"It has been for all our sakes."

"Oh, you always took sides for one another. And what can it matter to you, anyway? You are not hoping for a splendid match. What can you lose by returning to Havard Hall? Why, sometimes I believe you would not care." Tears filled the lovely eyes and rolled unchecked down her face.

"Well, it seems we are not to suffer banishment after all, Penny, so wipe your tears and stop worrying."

"How can I? It seems we must choose between being thrust summarily out of society and having to endure that . . . that awful old woman."

The next day Georgina was almost inclined to agree with

Penelope's opinion of their guest as she was called to Lady Dorothea's bed-chamber and forced to submit to the minis-trations of a barber sent for by that dame, who sat and watched while her maid covered her grey stubble with a freshly dressed wig. He was the most expensive in London and called only upon the grandest folk. Georgina sat and tried not to fidget as he snipped until she felt she surely must be bald.

"*Voila!*" cried the barber as he laid down his scissors. "*Regardez, madamoiselle!*"

Georgina regarded and was agreeably surprised. Her hair was now very short and curled naturally close to her head, revealing its boyish shape. Her cheekbones seemed higher, and the delicacy of her pale skin was shown to advantage.

"Thank you," she murmured. "*Merci, monsieur.* You are truly an *artiste*."

He acknowledged the compliment with a bow which at once expressed his appreciation and his awareness of his own genius.

Lady Dorothea dismissed him with a wave of her hand and commanded Georgina to, "Follow me!"

For the next three days she was taken from modiste to milliner—from hosier to shoemaker. When Lady Dorothea was informed by scandalised vendors that young ladies wore white for evening dances she over-rode them. She demanded, and was given, gowns of green, blue and gold, which Georgina tried on with head-spinning profusion. She ordered pelisses of velvet and fur, hats to match with brilliantly dyed feathers, muffs and reticules to accompany them. She sat upon tiny chairs, her bulk threatening their imminent collapse and bought evening gowns of silk and satin, and spangled stoles. She wore high red-heeled shoes with jewelled buckles, yet seemed aware that fashion called for the daintiest of low slippers for evening and elegant boots and half-boots for walking.

"Ma'am, no more, I beg," beseeched Georgina at the end

of the second day. "You have not once considered my sister. It is not fair."

"Penelope has her mother to care for her. I collect it is you who needs attention, and you are going to receive it."

The afternoon of the third day found them in a jeweller's emporium, where trays of exquisitely glittering and expensive pieces were paraded.

Ignoring Georgina's protestations, Lady Dorothea purchased and presented her with a necklace of orange garnets set in silver, with matching eardrops. To these, she added a breast ornament in the form of a bouquet of flowers of enamelled gold set with small diamonds, and a spray brooch of sapphires in silver.

Georgina could protest only on grounds of cost, because the Dowager Countess happily showed the most excellent taste in rejecting anything not charmingly becoming to a young lady.

Then, bowing low, the jeweller opened a small box and displayed a large and beautiful single opal in a simple gold setting, suspended from a plain gold chain.

"Ah, yes, the opal," murmured Lady Dorothea. "It is indeed lovely. Please add it to the other purchases."

"Ma'am, you cannot," whispered Georgina. "Such a gem must be very costly."

"And will suit you admirably," declared Lady Dorothea with satisfaction, "and I think that will do—for now."

Georgina could not help but revel in the loveliness she now so unexpectedly owned. She smoothed her hands over the soft, rich materials, and she and Jenny watched the opal flash deep fire in the candlelight. Georgina was as ingenuously delighted as Jenny. There was no doubt that the Countess's instinct was not at fault in her choice of style for Georgina, who held her newly modelled head with a proud tilt which became her.

The Dowager had lost no time in summoning Peregrine to her bed-chamber, from which he had emerged white with fury at her scathing remarks, but weak with the relief of being assured that his creditors would be satisfied.

He told Georgina how his protests had been over-ruled. "I cannot allow a woman to face this on my behalf," he had argued at first. "Some of those men to whom I owe money are quite unsuitable for you to meet."

"Stupid young jackanapes," replied Lady Dorothea without animosity, "to imagine I should so demean myself. This affair will be put into other more qualified hands than mine. I am but a medium for a man of business."

She had almost taken over the running of the household, bullying Mrs. Havard and the domestics, who astonished their mistress by showing no signs of revolt. They seemed to enjoy being ordered around by an autocratic countess, and even the temperamental cook had rhapsodised about her understanding of his need to produce creations, she instructing him to spare no expense in his future shopping.

Invitations to attend an evening party in Lady Dorothea's honour had been sent to half of London. She had made out the lists, and everyone had accepted. Those who were unasked were loud in their declarations that they should not like to be seen in the dwelling of a family about whom there had been disquieting rumours, before retiring home to rail against the injustice of their lives and to hatch schemes which might obtain for them a coveted invitation.

Penelope found it difficult to bite back jealous words at the sight of her sister's new finery, and Mrs. Havard was indignant that her beautiful favourite had not been singled out for Lady Dorothea's attentions. Only their respect for that dame's acid tongue kept them silent before her, though together they commiserated about the waste of money spent on such an unpromising girl as Georgina.

Consequently they were startled when, on the evening of the fifth day after the Dowager's arrival, Georgina appeared at the dinner which was to precede the party.

Jenny had taken ecstatic joy in dressing her mistress in a

Grecian gown of sea-green silk with an overdress of diaphanous golden gauze. The opal gleamed against her white skin, while in her glossy brown curls she wore a simple diadem of pale yellow silk roses. Her cheval glass told her she had never looked so well, and after dinner, when the guests began to arrive, she stood beside her mother at the head of the staircase leading to the main drawing room, watching with secret amusement the sudden recognition on the faces of her acquaintances.

Then her humour died as she saw a familiar figure making his way upstairs. His lordship, Alexander Earl of Rivington contrasted strongly with most of the other men in their costumes which outdid the ladies in brilliance. His white marcello waistcoat, white stockings and cream breeches were set off to perfection by his only concession to colour, a cloth coat of deep claret and a single ruby which glittered on the hand he held out to Georgina as he rose from his bow.

She felt deeply agitated. She had supposed he would have been sent an invitation, but that he should have accepted was a shock. Surely, after what had passed between them, he should have had the decency to stay away from her, at least for a while.

As he showed no sign of moving along the reception line until she acknowledged him, she felt forced to place her hand in his. He raised it to his lips and kissed the fingers in the soft kid glove, then gave her a look which told her he guessed exactly what she was thinking before he passed on.

She was hard put to conceal the tumult inside her as Sir Stannard Morton arrived, a vision in red velvet and gold lace, his pudgy fingers a riot of gems, and lingered in his greeting of Penelope who simpered in approved fashion and fluttered her lashes over her fan.

Miss Charlotte Ingram, accompanied by the elderly cousin who chaperoned her, floated up the stairs in a cloud of silver gauze, her jewels a wonder of filigrée gold and diamonds. Georgina stole a look at her brother, whose face showed all the secrets of his yearning heart as he greeted the girl he loved.

If Miss Ingram read him correctly she gave no sign, paying him scant attention, and Georgina was saddened to see how Peregrine's eyes followed her. He had no chance, she was sure, of capturing that lovely prize. It was true that Lady Dorothea had saved them from ruin, but she could hardly be expected to continue to pay for their pleasures in London indefinitely, and it could not be long before they returned home.

Georgina felt a surge of irrational anger towards Miss Ingram. Perhaps if it were not for her Peregrine would not have been tempted to increase their fortune. Why had he to fall in love with the unattainable? And why had she to follow his example?

Later, sitting alone in a side parlour where she had retired to sort out her turbulent thoughts, she was forced to admit that when the dark head of Alexander Rivington had been bent toward her she had a fleeting impulse to stretch out her hand and stroke it. She burned with shame at the thought, and wondered if that knowing look had encompassed that too. She had no wish to give him any further opportunity to torment her. She thought of his proposal of marriage, which had contained not a word of affection; perhaps his childhood experiences had destroyed his capacity for devotion. She pitied the woman he would one day marry—such a creature would live her life in terror of offending him and drawing upon herself his cutting satire. Then she remembered his kisses and trembled at the realisation that she ached to be held once more in his arms.

In an effort to shake off such abortive longings she jumped to her feet and hastened into the drawing room, where Lady Dorothea, a marvel of purple brocade enthroned upon a wide chair brought down from the attics for her use, was holding court.

Penelope need not have worried. Society was accepting the

Dowager Countess at her own estimation of her worth. Lord Rivington lounged at her side holding her fan, leaving both her hands free to gesticulate as she described the horrors of her journey north.

"Surely seven days upon the road from Gloucester is somewhat prolonged, even at this time of year," protested Sir Francis Calland.

"Not at all, young man. One should not neglect to call upon one's friends when given an opportunity, even though my visits were necessarily short. This seemed an excellent idea to me."

Sir Stannard gave his high-pitched laugh. "And to them also, madam, that I vow. Did they kill the proverbial fatted calf for you?"

"That they did, though I left home at such short notice that one letter apprising the family of my arrival had not reached there before I did myself and their amazement at my sudden descent upon them may be imagined."

Georgina had a vision of a country squire looking from the window of some quiet manor to see the imposing procession with which Lady Dorothea travelled, and her eyes gleamed in wicked joy. She turned aside to hide her mirth and almost collided with Lord Rivington, who had handed the fan to Sir Francis and whose eyes held an answering sparkle.

He bowed. "May I be permitted to congratulate you on your appearance, Miss Havard. Your cousin, Lady Dorothea is, I collect, responsible for freeing you from the conventional shackles which bind young ladies into wearing what does not become them."

Why did he *always* make the remarks which would most irritate her? She wanted to hurl angry words at him. To explain that she was dressed now as she would have chosen given the chance and money. Yet such a response would seem both childish and ungrateful to the Dowager Countess. Her enjoyment of the party left her and she felt a little sick.

"I had not expected to find you here tonight, sir."

"Had you not? Now why was that, I wonder."

"After what passed between us . . ." She bit her lip angrily. Whatever she said would be tauntingly construed by this man she was sure. Why had she not possessed enough wit to ignore the past—to gloss lightly over disquieting events as all the women around her seemed capable of doing?

The Earl bent his lean dark face towards her. "You are beautiful when you are angry, though I recall I have said as much to you before."

She gasped. Were there no limits to his effrontery? "You seem to take a pride in humiliating me. I daresay the rest of your life is well-matched to your treatment of me. I can only suppose that your pleasures lie in cruel sports, boxing no doubt, cock-fighting, bull-baiting and . . . and . . ." Her invention failed her, as she had little real knowledge of the world of a gentleman of fashion.

The Earl gave her accusations grave consideration. "I am reckoned," he stated finally, "to be a boxer of distinction, being given the honour, on occasion, of standing in the ring with Gentleman Jackson, something he accords only to a favoured few. As for cock-fighting, I confess to having participated in my erring youth; it seems to me that contestants with an equal chance can be enjoyed."

"It is a barbarous practice," flashed Georgina.

"I do not attend cock-pits since I reached the years of discretion," he protested. "And bull-baiting, I think you said."

"I suppose you are about to defend that too."

"You suppose wrongly, my dear Georgina. I have already said I favour contestants with equal chances. I do not consider that chaining a bull to a ring in the ground and subjecting it to be torn to pieces by savage dogs to be at all an edifying spectacle. I did not do so even in my misspent youth."

Could she never give him a set down? She blurted irrelevantly, "I did not give you permission to use my name, sir."

"Ah, then I apologise, as I would for mentioning the brutalities of gentlemen's sport, but I believed I need not class you with other females of my acquaintance, but accept you on your own terms."

His words sounded insulting, yet there was nothing in them to which she could rightly object. He was only following the line she had laid.

Abruptly he changed the subject. "Miss Ingram is a joy to watch in her manipulation of her suitors, do you not agree, Georg—I beg your pardon . . . Miss Havard?"

She followed his gaze and was chagrined to see Charlotte Ingram seated on a carved bench, the centre of an admiring throng of young men which included Sir Francis and Peregrine. She was doubly irritated to see that Miss Ingram appeared to be flirting outrageously with Sir Francis and taking a spiteful pleasure in Peregrine's unease, glancing at him sometimes with a look as amused as it was malicious. She was wishing there were some way she could interfere when she heard her name called in an imperious summons by Lady Dorothea.

"You are reckoned to be an original," stated the Dowager, "so what say you on the matter of whether or not one should bring serious subjects into the drawing room?"

"It seems to me," stated Georgina flatly, "that trivial conversation is the backbone of polite society. Where should we be without it?"

She had spoken in sincerity and was astonished when her words were greeted with a burst of delighted laughter and applause from the company.

"Your wit almost surpasses your charms," simpered Sir Stannard. Georgina was subjected to a glare from Penelope. It seemed that whatever she did or said was likely to be misunderstood by someone.

"You appear a trifle flustered," said the gently modulated tones of Sir Francis. "May I be permitted to take you for a little refreshment?"

She agreed gratefully. Charlotte Ingram had now, it

seemed, admitted Perry into her favour, and Sir Francis was not a man to dangle attendance where he was not made entirely welcome.

She sat down in the smaller room which was being used for supper and accepted a glass of ratafia. Sir Francis seated himself beside her and twirled his glass so that his red wine turned in a glowing spiral in the light of the many candles.

"Lady Dorothea can be a trifle overpowering, can she not?" he remarked.

"I find her so," confessed Georgina. "She seems to have taken over our lives. Though in all gratitude, I have to say that she has been immensely kind—to me in particular, though I cannot tell why."

She thought she surprised a speculative look on the handsome face beside her, but it was gone too fast for her to be sure.

Sir Francis continued to speak. "She is a woman who takes a fancy to one or another, then drops them when they bore her. She once played me just such a trick. You must know that she and I are distantly related. She gave me distinctly to understand that she would be responsible for certain debts. Then, when I needed her, she closed her purse, and I was forced into a most humiliating position. I had to beg for help from a source which I had rather not approach."

Georgina felt bewildered. Was he trying to warn her against trusting the Dowager? When she considered all the extra bills which were accumulating, many as a direct result of that grand dame's stay with them, she shivered. She remembered what her mother had told her of the allowance Sir Francis received from Lord Rivington and wondered if that was the unwelcome source to which he referred. If so, she could well understand his reluctance. He had probably got a tongue-lashing with the extra funds.

She spoke tremulously, unwilling to criticise Lady Dorothea, who was acting so well toward them. "My cousin does not seem to be a woman of fleeting fancies; she seems of a most forthright disposition. I beg your pardon, sir, if I seem to doubt your word, but . . ."

Sir Francis laughed. "I am rightfully reproved, Miss Havard. It would be entirely wrong for you to judge someone without proof."

Then his face became grave and he set down his glass. "Yet I must say what I feel. We are friends, are we not, you and I and Peregrine, and my knowledge of my family tells me that Lady Dorothea, although possessing a fortune which enables her to live in comfort, has not, to my belief, the means to travel in the grand style, nor to pay the large sums we both know of."

Involuntarily Georgina's hand went to the opal at her throat and Sir Francis's eyes did not miss the gesture. His tones were smooth. "I did not refer so much to the presents which she has made you, but to the moneys she has paid on your brother's behalf. The amounts were prodigious."

"Is there no-one in London who is ignorant of Peregrine's indiscretions?"

"Possibly they are not generally known for sure, but your brother has favoured me with his confidence. Believe me, I tried often to caution him."

"That was kind of you, sir," exclaimed Georgina, "if only Perry had been guided by you."

They returned to the large drawing room, which was now so crowded as to make movement a matter of some difficulty and ensured that Lady Dorothea's evening party would be described as a Crush and therefore an Enormous Success.

Miss Ingram was seated not far from the door, and Peregrine had found a chair by her side. He looked happy as she favoured him with smiles and words which evidently pleased him.

"Peregrine makes progress with the lovely Miss Ingram," murmured Sir Francis. Something in his tone made Georgina glance sharply at him. He looked as urbane as always as he gave her a bow. "Pray excuse me, ma'am, there is a matter to which I must attend."

He sauntered to the couple and engaged Miss Ingram in conversation, while Peregrine's face darkened with annoyance at the interruption.

Georgina stood hesitant, watching them. She could not hear their words, but it was clear that each man resented the presence of the other. Surely Sir Francis had no designs on the beautiful heiress. She would never be prepared to marry a man without a fortune to match her own so he could not have high hopes. And certainly Perry could not constitute a serious rival. Yet she felt a sudden irrational fear for her brother. Sir Francis was older and far more adept in the ways of the world, and he was looking at Peregrine now as he talked with Miss Ingram with an air of catlike vigilance. Then Georgina shook herself and told herself she was behaving foolishly. Flirting was an accepted part of society; no doubt all three of them knew and accepted the rules of the game.

She made her way back to Lady Dorothea, who was now amusing the company with tales of highwaymen.

"Travel today is not what it was." She gave an exaggerated sigh. "How can any of you younger folk imagine the thrill it was to be held at pistol point by a man like James Maclaine. They called him the Gentleman Highwayman, and many a fine lady entertained him in her home. Before he was hanged at Tyburn he was visited in Newgate prison by half London. How I wept when he died. He could have been a different man had he gained the wealthy bride he craved. Why, I myself would have wed him had my father allowed it."

"She must have been a precocious child," murmured Lord Rivington in Georgina's ear. "She was aged only ten years when that rascal died."

Georgina turned and saw his lordship's grey eyes were once more shining with amusement. For an instant she wanted to laugh, but she crushed her impulse to respond, and a mixture of the excitement of the past days, worry and fear for her brother, and the recently acquired terror lest Sir Frances should prove right about Lady Dorothea suddenly boiled up inside her. She said the first words which came into her head.

"How dare you mock her," she stormed. "She is old and should be allowed her pleasure without denigration. But it is like you . . . so like what I have come to expect from you to behave so unkindly."

"You thought me unkind?" All amusement had left his eyes, which were now as sharply cold as flint. "I did not mean my words to sound so. I would not have spoken had I not believed you to be a person who possessed a sense of the absurd that might allow you to laugh at someone even while respecting her."

The fact that he had read her character with such truth only inflamed her rage. Even while part of her recognized the injustice of her behaviour she continued, "I do not believe, Lord Rivington, that you ever stop to consider the feelings of others. You take delight in hurting those about you. You, sir, have a streak of . . . of vicious cruelty."

Surrounded as they were by chattering people she had kept her voice low, but several caught the angry tones and looked round in surprise. Georgina stopped speaking as she saw the curiosity in looks being directed their way. She had no wish to become the butt of their humour.

Lord Rivington was well aware of being observed. He held out his arm in an unspoken invitation to her to accompany him to some more quiet place, but she shook her head.

He stood looking at her a moment longer, and there was an expression in his eyes which both puzzled and disturbed her. She sensed, rather than saw, that many others had become aware of their quarrel. A smile, however forced, the placing of her hand upon his arm, would have closed the incident, but the bitterness of her anger almost choked her and again she shook her head. She heard the murmurs of the people around them, and there was a nervous high-pitched titter from Sir Stannard before Lord Rivington spoke quietly.

"As you will, madam. I had not thought you to be an ungenerous woman."

Then with a bow which was swift, but lacked nothing in courtesy, he was gone and Georgina, walking away from the now silent watchers, thought that his lordship would not easily forgive her for having made him look ridiculous.

CHAPTER *9*

She felt suddenly overcome with regret and sadness and longed to go to her room to shed the tears which hurt her throat and stung behind her eyes, but she could not retire from a party in her own home without excuse.

She walked dazedly towards her mother with the idea of saying she had the headache and asking if she might go to bed. She found Mrs. Havard supremely happy. Lady Dorothea's presence had opened doors which she had not thought to enter; promises of invitations for the future were being poured upon her, and she had obtained the certainty of the coveted Vouchers for Almacks for her girls. She was certain that Sir Stannard would soon come to the point of proposing marriage to Penelope, and even Georgina had turned out to have a surprising attractiveness.

Georgina decided not to spoil her mother's joy in any way, but to see the party through. She engaged in conversation with guests and applauded when musical young ladies gave renderings of popular pieces on the pianoforte, but by the time the entertainment began to break up her head was aching in truth, and she craved for rest.

The last few guests were leaving the hall and Georgina was about to climb the stairs to the upper chambers when she saw Peregrine leave his room, dressed in a cloak.

As he reached her she said, "Surely you don't intend to go out, Perry."

He laughed, but there was no joy in the sound. "Whyever should I not? It is not far past one o'clock. I have not been so early in my bed for many a night."

"Don't go, Perry, please."

He gently pushed her hand from his arm. "You are being foolish, sister. My friends would think me an odd fellow if I did not meet them."

"Make some excuse; stay at home tonight."

He stared at her. "What is it, love? Has someone upset you?"

"No . . . no, not really. I have an apprehension about you . . . I cannot explain. Perry, where are you going?"

"Only to play at cards. Now does that satisfy you?"

"I suppose it will have to. But . . . but you won't be seeing Sir Francis again tonight, will you?"

Peregrine flushed. "Why do you ask?"

"I don't know. I did not dislike him till tonight, then . . ."

"Has that man insulted you?"

She was startled by his vehemence. "Why, no, he has done nothing, said nothing, to which I can take exception. It is only an instinct I have, a mere feeling . . . I am worried, yet cannot tell why."

"Feminine vapours." He had meant his voice to sound teasing, but his attempt fell woefully flat.

"Oh, Perry, please try not to think any more of Miss Ingram."

Her brother's eyes glittered. "Why, Georgina, how odd that you too should give me a warning."

"What do you mean?"

"Only that Sir Francis saw fit to advise me that he has long made up his mind that Charlotte would marry him, and that in future I must leave her alone. He dared to presume! He has not the right, I am sure!"

"How do you know she has not given him the right? She is an abominable flirt."

"Georgina, I have warned you not to speak of Miss Ingram to me in that fashion, and since you will have the truth, yes, I do meet Sir Francis again tonight. I would not quarrel beneath my mother's roof, but I shall tell him exactly what I think of him. He imagines he can treat me as if I were a callow boy of no account—he shall learn differently."

He turned and flung out of the house, ignoring her pleas.

The guests had all left. Footmen were padding about, and the air was heavy with the acrid smoke of snuffed candles and the lingering scent of the perfume worn by both ladies and gentlemen. In the drawing room Georgina heard the distant murmuring voices of the others as they discussed the success of the party. She felt unable to talk to anyone else, and she fled to her room to find peace and seclusion. She needed to think.

But Jenny was awaiting her, having disobeyed orders to retire early, and Georgina could not disappoint her. She forced herself to chatter gaily to her maid of the evening's pleasures until at last, bed curtains drawn against the world, she was able to lay her throbbing head on the pillow. Now the tears would not come and she was denied their relief. And for a long time, till she finally slept, she seemed to hear the voice of Alexander Rivington as her brain echoed to his final thrust. "An ungenerous woman," he had called her and the memory was bitter because he had spoken the truth.

She awoke early, her head still aching badly and reached out to ring for Jenny, but stayed her hand. The girl had gone to bed very late and would be tired, and in truth, Georgina felt she could not endure anyone near her.

She slipped out of bed and pulled on a wrapper. Padding to her toilet table, she soaked a handkerchief in lavender water and returned to her bed, dabbing the cooling liquid on to her temple. But the pain did not cease, and she miserably recognised the approach of a migraine.

She thought about the laudanum drops her mother kept in her dressing room. Mr. Musgrove strongly disapproved of their use except in extreme cases, but Georgina, feeling suddenly unable to endure the torture of one of her rare violent headaches, resolved to seek the relief of the drops. Dim light was beginning to penetrate the curtains, and as she opened her door there were the distant sounds of servants preparing for another day.

She walked swiftly to the outer door of her mother's dressing room and was about to turn the handle softly when she heard the noise of a subdued commotion in the hall two floors below. She leaned over the stair rail and saw a sight which made her gasp. In the light of a branch of candles held by a footman her brother's face was for an instant clearly illuminated before he put up a hand to wave the light away. He was supported by another man, who said something in low tones. The footman sprang to open the door of a downstairs room, and as Georgina hurried to her brother she met the servant half-running to the room, bearing a bottle of brandy and a glass.

His mouth fell agape at the sight of his young mistress, garbed in a wrapper, her feet bare, then he tried to bar her way. "Don't go in there, miss, please, it ain't fitting . . ."

Angrily she brushed his arm aside and darted through the door. Perry was lying on a sofa, and kneeling by his side was Robert Kennerley. At her entrance he said without looking round, "Hurry with the brandy, man. Don't stand gaping like a damned fool . . ."

Peregrine's face was badly bruised, one eye nearly closed and the other about to follow its example. His mouth was cut and bleeding, and another trickle of blood came from his nose.

At her quick indrawn breath Robert turned. When he saw her, he leapt up and ineffectually tried to shield her brother from her gaze.

"George, I beg your pardon, I did not know you were

there. Please, do return to your bedchamber. Perry has had a little . . . encounter. It is nothing."

He glared at the footman, who said, "I tried to stop her, sir, but she would come in."

Perry groaned, and Georgina sprang to his side, "Leave me be, Robert, for heaven's sake, you idiot! Do you think I am like to faint at the sight of blood?"

He gave up his efforts to prevent her and she heard him berating the servant for his slowness as he poured a glass of brandy which he held to Peregrine's lips.

He groaned again. "My arm . . . my arm . . ."

Georgina took the glass from Robert's fingers. "Raise his head first," she commanded. "Do you want to choke him?"

Robert gave up all attempts to protest and did as he was bidden. Perry gasped as the raw liquid touched his cut lips, but as he sipped, some colour returned to his pallid cheeks.

"Bring warm water and cloths," snapped Georgina over her shoulder to the footman, who scurried to do her bidding. He recognised authority when he met it, although as he later remarked to his fellows in the kitchen, "I never before saw a young lady of quality behave in like manner. It weren't fitting—not fitting at all. She should have swooned as warrants her station."

Gently Georgina washed the wounds on her brother's face and gave no hint of her sick horror at the vicious cuts and bruises. She was discovering that tending the sick, however deep her sympathy, was not the same as seeing a loved one blood-smeared and torn. For an instant she had to fight off an attack of faintness and nausea, then raising her head she saw that her brother was staring at her from beneath puffy lids.

"George! What're you doing? No place for woman. Kenn'ley, take her 'way. My mouth—damnably sore—my arm . . ."

Georgina saw then that his arm was oddly twisted. She felt it with gently probing fingers, and he groaned.

"Is it broke?" Robert's voice betrayed his anxiety, and he gave an audible sigh of relief as Georgina shook her head. "But I think it is dislocated and must be put to rights before it becomes too inflamed. Do you know of a reputable surgeon?"

"No!" Peregrine's cry startled them both. "I'll not have this reach other ears. A stranger would be sure to pry, then all will come out. Surely I have been humiliated enough. George, you are forever talking of how you desire to be a medical woman. Cannot you attend me?"

She stood and looked thoughtfully at her brother. There was a lot about this affair which puzzled her, but Peregrine's agitation was so acute as to jerk him momentarily from his state of faintness. She had often assisted Mr. Musgrove and set limbs under his direction, but never on her own initiative.

Peregrine moved restlessly, "Georgina, for God's sake, begin and get it over with."

She turned to Robert. "Will you help me?"

"Certainly I will, in any way I can, but . . ."

"Do not argue, I beg," said Peregrine. "George knows what she is about."

She was touched and proud at his faith in her, but prayed inwardly that it was justified as she wielded the scissors to cut through his coat sleeve. He grimaced at the ruination of the expensive garment, but all was forgotten in his intense pain as she commanded Robert and the footman to seize his arm and extend it fully. He gave a smothered cry and swooned. Georgina, thankful for that mercy, pushed the elbow joint into position and bound her brother's arm with deft fingers.

"The worst is over, dear," she murmured as he regained consciousness. "Robert, pour brandy for us all. We have earned it."

Peregrine sipped the spirit, then asked weakly, "What o'clock is it?"

"Too late, old fellow," replied Robert. "We cannot hope

to reach Wimbledon in time, but you cannot be held to blame for that. Whatever possessed him, I cannot tell."

Georgina looked from one to the other. "What difference can it make as to the time? Surely, Robert, you would be better employed in going to a magistrate and trying to get the villains apprehended."

At the blank looks she received she stamped her foot. "The men who did this to my brother! They must be found and punished. He has been badly hurt. Did they take anything of value?"

Robert opened and closed his mouth and she looked at him helplessly. "Must I then do everything? Well, as soon as I have finished dressing his wounds . . ."

Turning to the footman she ordered, "Do you call my maid and request her to bring me the Yellow Basilicum Ointment she will find in the medical box in my room. Also a clean linen cloth and bandages I may use for a sling. Then I suppose I must go to see a law officer for myself."

"Y'don't understand," moaned Peregrine. "No magistrate . . . no one to know . . ."

"No one to know," repeated Georgina. "Are you then to suffer and allow the miscreants to run free?"

"Not villains," said Peregrine, "fair fight . . ."

"That it was not," cried Robert. "Fair fight indeed! Why, the man's studied insults were past all enduring. He acted intoxicated, but I vow he was not. I myself have seen him take much more wine than he did this night and remain cool as ice.

"He sneered and provoked you till you were goaded into striking a blow. Then instead of arranging matters as a gentleman should, he struck you back. He wanted you to fight. He desired to hurt you, knowing you stood no chance with him. Why, all London knows him to be one of the few men to have landed a facer on Gentleman Jackson. You are not evenly matched in weight or skill, and Rivington must be aware of it . . ."

Georgina felt sick. "Rivington?"

"You fool," groaned Peregrine. "Why must you let your tongue run on?"

"Did Lord Rivington attack my brother? Is that what you are saying?"

"Gentlemen's affairs," muttered Robert. "No need to fret yourself."

"Lord Rivington set on my brother, a stripling nowhere near him in weight and almost untrained in the so-called art of fisticuffs, and you tell me not to fret myself! I may be ignorant of gentlemen's affairs, as you call them, but I surely know that is not sporting.

"And you said something else I found puzzling. For what is Perry too late? Where was he going when this happened?"

At her words Peregrine half rose from the couch, then groaned and subsided. Georgina turned swiftly to him, gently holding him down by his shoulders. "Don't meddle, please, George . . . only make matter worse—must go—cannot be branded coward . . ."

Georgina said no more. Her brother's brow was becoming hot and damp, and she knew that she was unlikely to get any more information. Jenny came hurrying in and helped Georgina to rest his arm in a sling and tend his wounds with ointment and plasters. Then they watched him carried to his room, where they left his shocked valet, the footman and Robert to put him to bed.

Georgina then returned to her bedchamber, where she wrote directions for a light diet for Peregrine for Jenny to take to the kitchen and, after preparing a cooling draught for his use to ward off fever, she sank into the chair by her fire and allowed her tumultuous thoughts to invade her mind.

She doubted that either Peregrine or Robert would ever tell her the whole truth of what had happened, yet one thing was clear: the horrible damage to her brother had been inflicted deliberately by Alexander Rivington. Neither man had attempted to deny it once the fact had slipped out. From their jumbled words she had formed a picture of his lordship inciting Peregrine to fight, knowing him to be totally unfitted to oppose him.

Now that the excitement of the past hour had died down, the migraine which had been threatening seemed to explode inside her head, and she almost cried out with pain. She pressed a hand to her throbbing temple as she remembered the scene at last night's party and slowly a picture formed. She had humiliated Lord Rivington in public; that was something which surely had never occurred to him before and which he could not forgive. In his raging anger he had chosen to strike back at her in this brutal way. He knew of her love for her brother and was showing her that he had the means to punish her.

"He is wicked," she moaned, "vicious and cruel and I was right to spurn him. Marriage to him would be a living hell, so why did I learn to care for him? How has it happened? What kind of a woman am I?"

Tears of pain and misery rolled down her cheeks, and she knew that weeping would only increase her agony. When Jenny returned, she was all tender solicitude. She warmed her mistress's bed and insisted gently and firmly on her returning at once to it. Then, on her own initiative, she approached Mrs. Havard for some pain-relieving drops.

Georgina's mother, showing more kindness for her daughter now that she realised she could appear to advantage in society, actually brought the laudanum herself and administered it.

"What has happened to this household," she grumbled good-humouredly, "I have but now met Peregrine's valet, who tells me that his master is unwell and wishes not to be disturbed. I daresay he was up to some young man's prank last night."

After instructing Jenny to see that her mistress remained untroubled in any way, she returned to her own room, congratulating herself on her excellence as a mother.

The drops brought merciful relief, and Georgina slept. She awoke briefly to partake of light refreshment before sinking once more into a sleep from which she emerged early the next day to find, thankfully, that her headache had passed.

She threw back the bedclothes, tugged the bed curtain aside and put her feet to the floor, staggering a little at first. She sat in her wrapper before the fire, kindled earlier by some quiet little housemaid, and stared into the flames, trying to find a path through the maze of uncertainties.

So short a time ago her life had seemed ordered, and she had felt sure of where she was going. She wished with all her heart that Perry had not won any money, then he would still be at Oxford where he belonged and she would have continued in her uneventful way, tending the sick and possibly drifting into marriage with Luke Musgrove.

Even with the thought rose a tide of revulsion. She knew that never again would she be able to look upon the gentle apothecary with anything stronger than friendship. In fact, she acknowledged bitterly, she was spoiled for any man but the one in all the world she could never bring herself to marry.

Well, at least Penelope might emerge from the season safely attached to a rich husband. Georgina gave a little grimace as she thought of Sir Stannard, but felt sure that her lovely, empty-headed little sister would find all her wants fulfilled by him.

The door opened and Jenny came in walking softly toward the bed. Catching sight of her mistress, she gently remonstrated, "You should have rung, miss. I've been that worried about you."

"Thank you, Jenny, but there was no need. I have the headache sometimes, but it does not last long, and today I am quite recovered. How is my brother?"

"Fretting at being kept abed, Bendish says, but he feels

too bruised to stir so at present is being obedient to your orders."

Georgina smiled. "Good. I'll go to him soon, but first I'll take a little bread and butter and tea, please, Jenny. I feel I could eat something."

"Well, I'm glad of that. What you took yesterday wasn't enough to keep a sparrow alive."

After her light meal, Georgina dressed in a morning gown of dark blue chintz and slipped quietly along the corridor to Peregrine's room. The door was opened by a worried-looking valet, who seemed relieved at the sight of her.

"How has he fared? How is he this morning? I am so sorry to have left you to bear the burden, but I have been unwell myself."

"Yes, miss, so I was informed by Jenny. I have watched over him with great care. Towards the early hours he showed signs of a fever so I dosed him with the cooling draught, and I am pleased to say that he is now sleeping peacefully once more."

Georgina felt thankful, but Bendish had not finished. "But what I say is that such a thing shouldn't happen—not no way. I have been in service all my working life, and never have I seen one gentleman cause such injuries to another— not at fisticuffs, that is. I've seen worse in duels, of course, but what I say is . . ."

"At present," pointed out Georgina kindly, "you are saying altogether too much. I desire you to conduct me to my brother."

Bendish snorted and parted his master's bed curtains. Peregrine slept peacefully, and Georgina assured herself that his forehead was cool.

She tiptoed away. "Thank you, Bendish. Have you indeed had no rest all night?"

"I felt it was my duty to watch, and furthermore I like my young gentleman, and what I say is . . ."

Again Georgina interrupted him. "Bendish, I must call

upon your further help. I may be too late as last night my headache drove my wits astray, but I would like this affair kept from Mrs. Havard for as long as possible. I daresay she will be bound to find out sooner than later, but she will be less shocked if my brother's wounds are not quite so obvious. I will have a word with Webster and rely on you to curb curiosity below stairs—that is, if I am in time."

Bendish snorted once more and drew himself up. "I hope I know my duty, miss. I took the liberty of commanding the footman's silence last night, Miss Havard, and there is no reason why any other servant should discover the truth of what happened, your maid Jenny being quite a superior young person and more able than most young women to keep a still tongue in her head."

"I am grateful to you, Bendish. Watch over him a little longer, if you will, and I will relieve you as soon as possible so that you may rest. You are a good friend to my brother, and I thank you most sincerely."

The valet's face went a dull red with pleasure, and for once he remained speechless while Georgina took the opportunity to slip away. After breakfasting late, Mrs. Havard and Penelope went for their customary drive in Hyde Park, and Georgina was able to sit with Peregrine while Bendish took some rest.

Her brother's face was blotched and swollen with bruises and cuts, and the yellow salve did nothing to improve the sight he presented. She watched him, her eyes glowing with subdued rage at Lord Rivington's behaviour. Surely he must feel some remorse for his action. Perhaps he truly had been the worse for wine—but Robert had been so sure that he was not. And for her brother to have a dislocated elbow showed that quite unnecessary force had been used against him. They must have wrestled as well as used fists. No, there could be no excuse for Rivington. Perhaps now he would have the decency to quit London for a time. She did not doubt that this latest scandal would have been circulating round the men since last night, and surely even the most ruthless of them could never condone such wanton brutality.

At a gentle scratching at the door she called "Enter," and was brought to her feet in astonishment at seeing Charlotte Ingram hurry into the room, her lovely eyes showing great anxiety.

"Forgive me, dear Miss Havard, I was forced to bribe a servant to show me the way, but I had to come. Where is he?"

"My . . . my brother . . . ?"

"Yes, yes, whom else should I mean? I have come here to see him. When I heard what had happened . . ."

"Just what have you heard—and how?" interrupted Georgina.

"I was told he had been severely injured and was like to die. As to how I learned . . . through servants' gossip. There were witnesses to the fight. Please do not look disgusted with me, dear Miss Havard. One always does learn of these matters through one's maid. In our station nothing can be kept hidden."

"So it would seem."

"Please," faltered Miss Ingram, "may I not see him before . . . before . . ."

She held a square of lace to her trembling lips, and Georgina said, "There is no need for such fears, ma'am. My brother is far from being so ill as you seem to suppose."

Charlotte sank into a chair. "Thank God. Oh, thank God. It was that devil Rivington, was it not? I am ashamed—I feel so much to blame."

"You? How so? In what way can you have been involved?"

Charlotte flushed, but looked up at Georgina bravely. "I think . . . the quarrel may have been caused by jealousy . . . over me. It has long been expected by our families and friends that Alexander and I should wed. At first I was quite willing—we understood one another, you see—I . . . ignored any of his little pleasures which . . . well, in short, we would never have obstructed one another's freedom, but I would have produced the heir he needs."

Georgina's face showed the distaste she felt, and Charlotte's cheeks grew redder. "It is an arrangement which many have to accept, ma'am." Then she sighed. "But you are right, of course, it was only when I learned to love truly that I knew I could not endure a loveless marriage. But I had not known that Alexander's feeling for me was any deeper than mine for him. He is so cold—so distant—how could I have known?"

Georgina's voice was icy. "Are you trying to tell me that he fought my brother over you?"

"I have heard there was mention of my name."

With a searing effort Georgina thrust away all the humiliating implications of Charlotte's words and asked, "But why are you here?"

Charlotte looked at her twisting hands. "I love your brother, Miss Havard. He is so . . . so very dear to me."

"But you have not given him to understand . . . you have flirted outrageously with others, and in his presence too."

Again Charlotte's lovely face was suffused with delicate colour. "I knew that Peregrine cared for me. A woman always knows these things, does she not? But he never spoke of his love, and a woman cannot institute such talk. I thought that by making him jealous . . ."

"I see. You are right, of course. Perry loves you deeply. He has spoken to me of his hopes. Yet he did not tell you? I can only suppose that his lack of fortune made him fearful. He has no money, Miss Ingram, none at all. I must tell you that we came to London only because . . ."

"Of the Lottery Tickets," finished Charlotte. "Yes, I know."

Now it was Georgina's turn to redden. "How? Does all the town know of it? Have we then been a subject of talk and . . . and amusement?"

"No, I am sure you have not. I was told by Sir Francis Calland. He spoke only as a friend to warn me against making an imprudent match. He could hardly be aware of how much more it endeared your brother to me, Miss Havard, knowing that he dared so much to give his sisters their chances."

Georgina said sharply, "Sir Francis seems to make a habit of giving much friendly advice."

The two girls were silent a moment, then Charlotte asked in a small voice, "May I see him, please?"

Georgina was doubtful. "He is badly cut and bruised. I fear it would distress you. Besides, he is asleep . . ."

Peregrine's voice was weak, but filled with joy. "He is not asleep and has heard every word. Miss Ingram, Charlotte . . ."

Charlotte leapt up and pulled aside the bed curtains. "Oh, Peregrine, your poor face. My angel! What has that villain done to you?"

"He has been the best friend in the world if he has brought me you, my dearest one."

Georgina watched as Charlotte leant over and Peregrine put his good left arm about her shoulders and drew her close. Then she turned away, feeling that their first rapturous embrace was not for other eyes to witness. Her honesty compelled her to admit that even as she rejoiced in her brother's good fortune, she felt a wave of jealousy and pain that they should know such ecstasy while she had discovered yet another reason for not putting her trust in Lord Rivington.

How could he have been truthful in his protestations of his attraction to her while feeling so deeply over Charlotte that he was willing to fight over her? And to fight the brother for whom she cared so much. None of it made sense. She stood staring sightlessly out of the window until Charlotte rejoined her.

"He has promised to eat as much as possible and to rest again—for my sake. We both wish to be married, my dear

Georgina—I may call you that now, may I not, when we shall soon be sisters. As soon as Peregrine is recovered he is to call upon my father, who I am sure will give his consent. I will indicate to papa that I have found a man whom I truly love. And—Georgina—there is no need, is there for anyone but ourselves to know of my behaviour today. It was only because I believed my dearest Peregrine near to death that I behaved so indiscreetly."

Georgina nodded, then asked, "Can you be so certain that your papa will give his consent?"

"Oh, I believe he will. He has been berating me these past four years for not choosing a suitable husband, and Peregrine is entirely acceptable in all ways save that of fortune. And that need not concern us. My grandmama left me a large portion which will come to me on my marriage so long as I please my family. All will come safely about, Georgina, you will see. Papa can never refuse me anything I want for long."

Impulsively Georgina leaned forward and kissed Charlotte who smiled delightedly. Now that she understood Charlotte's behaviour she felt ready to welcome her into the family and thought she might prove a more congenial companion than Penelope.

"I shall long for affairs to run smoothly, Charlotte, and wish you and Peregrine all the happiness in the world."

CHAPTER *10*

By early evening of the following day word had reached Mrs. Havard that Miss Charlotte Ingram had come to the house to call upon Peregrine, and she was vociferous in her questions.

She insisted on visiting Peregrine, and after shrieking at

the sight of his blotched, bruised face, she began to sigh with amazed gratification that he should have sustained such injuries in defending the name of his beloved. She was ecstatic when she came downstairs. "Miss Charlotte Ingram," she breathed. "Peregrine will be most suitably settled. And when Sir Stannard hears that we are to be allied with so great a family, he will surely offer for Penelope. Indeed, I am persuaded of it. Miss Charlotte Ingram," she repeated, "the daughter of Baron Reed, the head of a most illustrious line and she an heiress—this is beyond all things delightful!

"Georgina, we must be sure that not a word of Peregrine's embarrassment leaks out. I know that Lady Dorothea has settled his debts, but we do not wish Baron Reed to think that our dear Perry is reckless, do we? Once they are married, all will be well."

Sir Stannard was as impressed by the whispered confidence as Mrs. Havard could have hoped. "My dear ma'am, you will be linking yourselves to one of the highest families in the land. Such a match will open doors in Court circles. Most gratifying; most gratifying, indeed."

He paid particular attention to Penelope during his visit and upon leaving pressed Mrs. Havard's hand warmly as he said, "You must keep me informed of the progress of Peregrine's expected bethrothal. I shall await your news with deepest interest."

"It is the spur he needed," declared Mrs. Havard when Sir Stannard's rotund form had disappeared from sight. "Girls, our fortunes are made. He will declare himself now, I know he will. Only let your brother's betrothal be announced in the *Morning Post* and soon we shall have another to insert."

Lady Dorothea said in tones of deep satisfaction, "It is indeed fortunate that I was able to come to town to rescue you all from poor Peregrine's entanglements. Once he and Penelope are respectably settled that will leave only Georgina, will it not, young lady?"

She gave Georgina the full benefit of her porcelain smile

and there was an expression in her face which puzzled the girl. It seemed almost expectant, and Georgina sensed the watchful stare on her back as she excused herself and hurried away from the probing of those hawklike eyes.

The Polite World buzzed with rumours of the new romance, and during the morning calls of the following day, Mrs. Havard entered drawing rooms with all the pride due to a woman whose children were about to capture two advantageous marriage prizes. At Lady Sarah's, enjoying the envy of less successful mamas, Georgina was wishing she could have thought of a reason for not accompanying her mother as she saw the maliciously pitying glances of some of the women who knew that Penelope would be setting up her own establishment first, when the doorway framed the figure of Lord Rivington. He was dressed with quiet elegance, but Georgina's immediate thought was that there was not a mark on him to show that he had been engaged in a brutal fight so short a time ago. Remembering her brother's pain and injuries, she clenched her hands until the nails dug into her palms.

The meaningful looks cast in the direction of her family, and the whispering behind fans, led her to believe that the news of the encounter had leaked out. But Lord Rivington seemed unaware, or perhaps uncaring, of the murmurs which followed him as he greeted his hostess, then sauntered with calm deliberation to Georgina and stood looking down at her.

She did not know what to expect. An apology? Some kind of excuse? She savoured phrases which would throw such words back into his face. She could hardly believe her ears when he bowed low and murmured, "You look delightfully, my dear Miss Havard."

Her anger became so tangible as to cause her almost a physical pain, and a flush rose to her cheeks. Conscious of the watchful eyes upon them, she bit back words and stared at the floor.

"It seems you are without your usual fluency," said the

Earl, who maintained his infuriating calm, "yet I feel, yes, I am quite sure, Miss Havard, that you have something you wish to say to me."

He held out his arm. "Pray allow me to walk a while with you. I know that Lady Sarah will excuse us should we explain that we desire to examine her vinery. She actually has a conservatory here, in London. I believe she is as fond of gardening as . . . as is another lady of my acquaintance."

Recalling her feelings of chagrin when she had humiliated the Earl before, Georgina rose and placed her hand upon his arm. Lady Sarah dismissed them with an indulgent smile, and Georgina allowed herself to be led to the end of the drawing room to a small door which opened into an extension built mainly of glass. The air was hot and a little steamy, and the enormous vine twined itself up the walls and over the ceiling shutting out the daylight so that it seemed to Georgina that she must be in one of the tropical jungles she had read about. She looked at the convolutions of the plant then into the eyes of Lord Rivington, whose mind she believed to be as devious and twisted as the vine.

"I was . . . excessively surprised to see you here."

"That is the second time you have expressed your surprise at my presence, Miss Havard. It seems to be my fate continually to amaze you."

His tones were light, his voice amused, and she let her eyes travel slowly over him, his fashionable coat which hid the muscular frame she knew to lie beneath, his hands so white yet with the strength of steel and caught her breath in a little sob.

"Have you no shame—no regret for what you have done to my brother? He is little more than a boy, while you . . ."

The grey eyes darkened. "Has that young fool told you what occurred then? I had not thought him stupid."

"No, he did not tell me. The news reached me by . . . by accident. I do not propose to explain . . ."

"Ah, then his friend, Kennerley allowed it to slip," said

the Earl dispassionately. "He always was a loose-tongued young idiot in his cups. And now you take me for a villain, is that it? You assume, as ever, the worst of me."

Georgina faltered. "Have I been misled? Was it not you who so cruelly attacked my brother. Who, if I am to believe my informant, provoked him into striking a blow which allowed you to . . . to . . ."

Her voice broke. She clasped and unclasped her hands. It was suddenly very important to her that he should prove her wrong. The Earl grasped both her hands in his and drew her to him. "I could not lie to you, my dear, even if I wished— which I do not. I was wholly responsible for your brother's injuries."

"But why?" She was pleading now, not only for an answer to her question, but for reassurance which would tell her that this man, whom she so longed to feel free to love, would be able to explain the incident to her satisfaction.

His arm slipped about her waist and he became serious as he said, "Can you not forget Peregrine and think of me? I tell you, Georgina, that I still hold to the offer of marriage I made you." His lips quirked a little. "Life with you might be exasperating, but I could be sure that it would never be dull."

She stood, his hands still holding hers, deeply conscious of the strength of his arm about her. She felt a shuddering need to press close to him, to feel his lips once more on hers, and shame flooded her.

"You may find it easy to forget those you have wronged," her voice was low and throbbing, "but I do not. You are a coward, sir."

There was an instant of utter stillness. She felt the sudden tension in him. Abruptly he released her and stepped back. "The names you call me are not pretty, madam. First it was 'libertine' and now 'coward.' I have called men out for less."

Georgina spoke deliberately. "The more so, perhaps, if they be inexperienced boys."

Again, there was a short, charged silence. "I cannot recall ever having called out any man whom I did not believe richly deserved a set-down and who was not perfectly fitted to meet me."

"How can I believe you? You do not deny that you have hurt my brother grievously."

"No, I do not deny that." A cold smile twisted the sardonic lips for a moment. "Yet, he lives to tell the tale. He will fight another day—as assuredly he would not have done if . . ."

"If you had fought a duel with him, as I must suppose to have been your original intention. I know something of the rules, you see. I know that if blows have been exchanged then no apology may be accepted before shots have been fired.

"But Peregrine is a hot-headed boy who forgot the rules. You could not have foreseen that instead of continuing the affair as a so-called man of honour should, he would return blow for blow. So you beat him unmercifully, deriving God knows what pleasure from it. If it was to take revenge for the way I treated you, why had you not the courage to insult and humiliate *me*? You appear to be much practised in the arts of wounding in every way."

She felt a flash of fear at the cold anger in his face, yet could not control her tongue. "I despise you, Lord Rivington, for the coward that you are. I hate and despise you!"

She almost flinched as he moved towards her, but his voice was soft. "Are you sure you hate me, Georgina?" He stepped closer to her and she backed away until she felt the knotted tendrils of the vine pressing into her back. He followed her, then his arms were about her, holding her helpless in an embrace which, for all her valiant words, she ached to return.

"Are you sure you hate me?" he asked again as his lips found hers and moved upon them, demanding a response which it took all her will to refuse. She would not show feeling to a man whom she was sure would use her as he used everything and everyone—as a diversion from the tedium of his life.

At last he released her, and she forced herself to look into his eyes. They were turbulent with some emotion she could not define before a shutter of indifference veiled their expression as he offered her his arm. "I will not apologise, Georgina. I beg your pardon, in the past few—fascinating— moments, I fear I have been forward. So, Miss Havard, I will not apologise. Not for what happened between Peregrine and myself, nor for kissing you again, as I have so often wanted to. Pray allow me to conduct you to your mama."

Pride kept her head held high and her lips smiling casually as they reentered the drawing room. Pride parried her mother's questions when they returned home, but her foolish heart had its way when she was alone, and she shed tears of misery and mortification. How was it possible to love a man for whom she had no respect? He was utterly despicable in all he did, yet she knew she wanted him with all her being.

At a scratching at the door, she called, "Enter." It would be Jenny, who would be soothing even if she knew nothing of the reasons for her lady's distress. She did not turn her head until the imperious tones of Lady Dorothea brought her to her feet.

"Madam . . ." she stammered.

"Don't you madam me," said the Dowager. "Your mama cannot discover what the world is waiting to hear, but I do not intend to leave this room without a straightforward answer from you."

"I do not understand . . . pray, will you not be seated?"

Lady Dorothea snorted her contempt for the tiny chairs which could not accommodate her wide skirts of bright blue-and-yellow-striped satin and sank onto the oak chest at the foot of the bed. "Now, sit yourself, miss, and be prepared to talk to me without dissembling."

Georgina did as she was bid and sank into a chair, clasp-

ing her hands to control their shaking. She guessed that the
Dowager was about to speak of this morning's events at
Lady Sarah's and hardly dared hope to hide her true feelings
from those needle-sharp eyes.

"I collect," said Lady Dorothea, "that you were closeted
with Alexander Rivington for some ten minutes today in
Lady Sarah's Vinery. No, do not interrupt—I have my information on good authority, so there is no use in denying
it."

"I was not about to deny it, madam."

Lady Dorothea frowned. "You are very pert. You will be
pleased to inform me when your betrothal to Lord Rivington
is to be announced to the world. I am desirous of returning
to my home. I mislike present day society on the whole and
find that most of the men are namby-pamby nincompoops.
There a some few exceptions, and Rivington is one of them.
You are indeed fortunate to be marrying him and not a
mincing, prancing fool like your silly sister has set her design
upon."

Georgina raised startled eyes. "But I am not to marry his
lordship, ma'am. I cannot think why you should have such a
notion."

"He has asked you to be his wife. Come now—no un-
truths with me, miss. They will avail you nothing."

"Lord Rivington has asked me to be his wife, and I have
refused him."

Lady Dorothea favoured her with her startling smile.
"Quite right and proper for a young lady. It is not seemly to
accept the first time. I remember I kept Lutterworth dangling—well, no matter. Alexander informed me that you had
not yet accepted him, but I had every expectation of your returning today an engaged woman."

Georgina sprang to her feet. "Are you telling me that you
have been discussing me with Lord Rivington—that you
knew he would be present today at Lady Sarah's—that he
would again insult me with an offer?"

"Insult you?" The Dowager's voice rose to a scream. "One of the richest men in England, from a line as old as royalty's, asks a chit without a fortune—*and* no looks to speak of—to marry him, and you term it an insult! Have you lost your senses? And please to sit down when I am addressing you, and stop fidgeting about."

Georgina's knees were trembling so much by now that she was glad to obey, but she said with quiet determination. "I refused Lord Rivington again today, and I tell you, ma'am, that I shall never marry him—never! Not in any circumstances whatsoever."

"What masquerade is this? He was so sure. Why, when he wrote to me of your brother's misfortunes, he gave me clearly to understand that you and he . . ."

"*He* wrote to you. Is that why you came to town? Is that why you are prepared to settle our financial difficulties—because *he* wrote to you . . . ?"

Lady Dorothea bit her lips. "I have said too much. It was all to be kept secret until after your marriage." She continued to speak as if to herself. "He seemed so sure, else why should have he assumed so great a responsibility?" She looked at Georgina. "Are you sure you have not given him reason to believe . . . ?"

She stopped abruptly as she saw a horrified awareness dawning in the girl's eyes. Shock had drained the colour from her cheeks and her eyes were enormous.

The Dowager held out her hands, and her voice was unexpectedly gentle. "Come here, child."

Blindly, Georgina stumbled to her and sank on to the chest beside her cousin, who put an arm about her. She spoke flatly. "Did he—Rivington—make it possible for us to remain in London? Is it to him that we owe so much?"

Lady Dorothea's voice was softer now than Georgina would have thought possible. "My dear, truly I thought it some kind of lover's ruse. I assumed you must be half aware of the facts. I am not a rich woman, my dear. I thought you knew. Now I see I was wrong: you knew nothing of the truth. But having guessed so much, I see I must explain it all to you.

"Alexander is a connection of mine—he is a member of my late husband's family, and he knew of my relationship with your father. When he wrote, telling me he had decided upon a wife, I was delighted. It has long been the ambition of those who care for him to see him respectably settled. He told me of Peregrine's indiscretions, which would have driven you from town before he could properly lay court to you —and he could not set the world by the ears by assisting you openly. He needed a female who could help without creating ill-natured speculation, and who better could he ask than myself to rescue you all?

"I must confess that when I heard of your brother's wildness I was forcibly reminded of Handsome Havard and his excesses, but Rivington assured me that the boy had been led astray. Alexander desired me to keep your family comfortably in London, without scandal, till he should have won you.

"My good child, I could not have settled Peregrine's enormous debts, nor supplied the money to maintain such a household as this as well as my own at home. I am merely an agent for Lord Rivington."

Still Georgina did not speak, and the Dowager took one of the girl's icy hands in hers. "Don't look so stricken, love. All will come happily about. It is not the first time, nor will it be the last, that a gentleman has saved his betrothed's family from embarrassment. What can it signify in the end?"

"I despise him utterly," said Georgina dully. "He is by far the most unscrupulous and ruthless man I have ever met. He seems to possess all the traits I most loathe, and his chief delight toward myself seems to lie in goading me about my ideals. Now you tell me we owe him debts we can never hope to repay."

"Such notions for a young unmarried gel! Well, he told

me you were not the usual style of society miss. I suppose that's why he wants you. It certainly ain't for your beauty or encouragement, that's clear."

"Sir Francis Calland warned me," said Georgina. "Why did I not listen? But what could I have done?"

"That's right," encouraged the Dowager. " 'Tis a wise women who recognises defeat when she meets it . . ."

"Rivington probably led Perry to his downfall," continued Georgina. "He knew it would make him desperate enough to accept your help without question."

"Well! You have some odd notions about a man whom I have always found to be honourable. But be that as it may. You see now that the sooner you stop your flirtatious behaviour and accept Alexander, the sooner we may all be comfortable again."

"I will not marry him!"

"You have no choice," said Lady Dorothea. "Georgina, my dear, ladies of our station must sometimes make sacrifices for the sake of their families. Think of Peregrine and Penelope . . . imagine their blighted hopes. Rivington holds your brother's vouchers. Debts of honour, Georgina."

"I do not believe Charlotte Ingram would reject Peregrine because he owes money," argued Georgina.

"Perhaps she might not wish to do so. As matters now stand, she will have her way with her papa because Peregrine is a man of birth and lineage, and Lord Reed desires to see his daughter married. She has refused so many offers. But should the full extent of Peregrine's activities become known —I collect he has been frequenting some most unsavoury gaming halls—I fear that the Baron will forbid all further contact between them.

"And there is Sir Stannard. I rather feel he might find a sudden call abroad if Penelope finds herself the sister of a disgraced man."

"Just now you intimated that Lord Rivington was a man of honour," pointed out Georgina. "You seem to have revised your opinion. Do you really believe him to be so callous that he would destroy my family's hopes?"

Lady Dorothea sighed. "Who can tell which way a reject-ed suitor will turn? And he is a proud man—unused to be crossed."

"I will not marry him," Georgina said again.

"But you owe it to him, and now I have explained . . ."

"Yes, you have explained, madam, that I and my family owe him a good deal. Well, he shall be paid. For I will go to him and offer myself to him. But I will not tie myself for life to such a one as he. When . . . when he has had his fill of me—and I have reasons for knowing that will not take long —I will return to the life I had mapped out for myself. No, not quite that, for of course I would never be able to marry."

Lady Dorothea peered into Georgina's face. Her own had paled beneath the maquillage. "You've been to the theatre too often, my girl. Ladies of birth do not 'offer' themselves, as you somewhat coarsely phrase it. I don't blame you for your resentment, as it seems you were truly deceived, but you've said your piece and now let us be done with charades. Try to remember that Alexander Rivington is most wonder-fully wealthy and highly placed, and that his person is unex-ceptionable. I will go to him now and tell him that you will marry him at the end of the Season."

Georgina stood and faced the Dowager. "No, ma'am, you will not do so. I will go to him myself. But I will not marry him."

Lady Dorothea's face lost its pallor, and she purpled with fury. "Your father was a damned fool, your mother is too, and that sister of yours follows them both, but I had high hopes of you. Any girl who can capture Rivington must, I believed, be a rare creature indeed. But you shall not shame your family. I will go at once to acquaint your mama with the facts, and you shall be locked in, miss, do you hear, locked in on bread and water until you regain your senses."

She struggled to her feet, her panniers swaying as she

stalked to the door, but Georgina was there before her. She swung it open, slipped through with the cries of the infuriated Dowager resounding in her head before they were muffled as she slammed shut the heavy door, turning the solidly fashioned key in the lock. Then she flew downstairs and out into the road.

She ran almost the length of Upper Brook Street before she noticed the attention she was attracting. One or two servants on errands gave her curious stares, and a roughly dressed man carrying a pedlar's basket whistled insolently through his teeth. She realised what an odd sight she must present, dressed as she was in a cinnamon velvet morning gown. The light April breeze ruffled the white lace at her wrists, and she felt thankful at least that her gown was plain. If her mother had had her way, she must have made her escape in floating white draperies.

She felt impelled to go on. What a fool she had been to tell Lady Dorothea of her intention. Why had she not controlled her unruly tongue and made her plan in secret? Yet she knew she could not have carried out her purpose in cold blood. Anger burned in her as she hurried on. She had never entered Lord Rivington's town house, but no one in Polite Society had not heard of the Earl's magnificent mansion built in the previous century in the newly established Grosvenor Square.

Reaching the end of Upper Brook Street she paused and looked about her, recalling suddenly that she did not know the exact whereabouts of the Earl's house. The square looked bigger than ever, and she walked slowly, staring at front doors, despairing of reaching her goal before she should be stopped.

Her rage and sense of debasement were like inner fires driving her on. All the Earl's insults and torments of the past weeks whirled in her brain, and her only desire now was to pay her family's debts and free herself forever from his power.

She had walked the length of one side of the square when

two young men left one of the houses and stared at her before approaching her. She knew neither of them, but they, seeing her without cloak, bonnet, or escort, stopped and mockingly raised their hats. She had assumed them to be about to offer their assistance till she looked into their faces. Their smiles were lascivious, their glances raked her person and lingered on the white skin above the low-cut neck of her gown, then one stepped close and slid an arm about her waist.

She tried to push him away, which amused them both. "Come now, little one," said the man who held her tight, "here are two who are willing to share your favours and pay handsomely. Forget whoever you were seeking."

She struggled desperately, "Sirs, you are mistaken . . ."

Then, from the corner of her eye, she saw a door further along open and a well-known figure in a caped driving coat walk down the steps, drawing on a glove as he did so. He turned and frowned at the scuffle, then his eyes widened for an instant before he came quickly over.

"Your pardon, gentlemen, the lady does not require your attentions."

The two young men turned to bluster, then recognising the Earl, stammered their regrets. "A thousand pardons, sir. Give you good-day, ma'am. Why did you not explain?"

They winked at her before walking laughingly down the street.

Lord Rivington stared at Georgina as she fought to regain a measure of composure. "You must not think hardly of them," he said, mildly, "seeing you dressed so, walking alone, they assumed . . ."

"I am aware of what they assumed," flashed Georgina. "Like all you fine men, they imagined any woman who was not surrounded by a protective wall to be theirs for the taking."

The dark eyebrows rose, but the grey eyes were gentle as the Earl said, "You are in some kind of trouble, Miss Havard? May I be of service to you?"

"You!" She invested the word with all the cold contempt she could muster, and his face grew cold.

"I am to assume, then, that you have discovered something to my further discredit. But surely you cannot have left your home attired like that simply to abuse me once more."

"No, sir, I have not. I have come to . . . to . . ."

She could not go on. To her fury she felt her throat constrict with tears. She had suddenly remembered that the dress she wore, her dainty kid shoes, the delicate brooch of silver and diamonds pinned at her breast had all been paid for with his money. She thought of how she and her family had been duped to amuse this arrogant man, and she felt utterly vulnerable in her humiliation.

Lord Rivington took her elbow and led her unresisting to his house. A knock brought to the door a stately butler who quickly hid his astonishment.

"This lady has met with a—mishap," blandly explained his lordship.

He piloted Georgina into a book-lined room, where she sank into a carved chair and accepted a glass of wine. Her throat eased, and she looked at the Earl, who was gazing out of the window into the quiet square. She sought for words with which to express herself. How soon, she wondered, would the door resound with frantic knocking as someone came searching for her? The thought spurred her on. If Perry believed she was a victim of Lord Rivington, he would surely challenge him, and that must never happen. Later, somehow, she would find a way to pacify her brother, but at present he was still bitterly angry with the Earl.

"I have something to say to you, my lord." She spoke icily, hating the nervousness which caused a slight tremor in her voice.

He moved to stand before her, inclining his dark head courteously.

"I have discovered from Lady Dorothea that you . . .

that you are responsible for bringing her to town—using her as a shield to put us hopelessly at your mercy . . ."

She was interrupted by a mild curse from the Earl. "I thought that Cousin Dorothea could keep a still tongue in her head. It seems I was badly mistaken."

"You had no right," burst out Georgina.

"I had to act swiftly. How would you have reacted had I offered help openly. You would, perhaps, have enjoyed seeing your brother in a debtors' goal, Miss Havard, maybe even joined there by the rest of you. I did what I believed best in the circumstances."

"Circumstances which you no doubt engineered. My brother was led into gaming hells, of that I am sure."

He did not answer at once. Eyes like flints bored into hers. When he spoke, his voice was soft. "Your opinion of me never fails to amaze me, my dear Miss Havard."

She shivered at the menace in his tones, but found the courage to proceed. "You have placed us in an intolerable position. My mama can never repay what we owe to you."

"I do not consider your family to owe me anything. I acted as I did from a wish to help you. Surely Lady Dorothea explained."

"Certainly she did. She told me how the great Lord Rivington set his fancy on me and planned a campaign to buy me in a despicably underhand fashion."

"I see." The Earl's mouth was grim. "And now you have discovered my secret you feel, naturally, that you can accept nothing further from me. Yet your presence here would indicate that you have much to say to me that cannot wait. Maybe one more small favour to ask. Pray, do not hesitate. Anything I have is yours."

"You know what is close to my heart, my lord. It is my sister's and brother's happiness. I cannot pretend to comprehend your motives for first helping Peregrine and then hurting him so badly, but I do ask you, sir, to allow his courtship of Miss Ingram to proceed smoothly. They truly love one another."

"But of course. And the matter of Miss Penelope and Sir Stannard?" His tone spoke only polite boredom, yet she became aware of something deeper in his eyes.

"Penelope is awaiting Sir Stannard's proposal. All the world knows that. Should anything occur to . . . well, she would be deeply distressed."

"Ah, yes. Love sometimes assumes curious guises, does it not? But tell me, Miss Havard, why do you not dissemble? Keep me dangling as a suitor until your brother and sister have captured their prizes in the marriage market? Then your mama would have only to apply to her wealthy relatives to settle all her debts."

"How can I know if you would hold off so long? After the way you treated Peregrine you can scarcely expect me to trust you?"

"I see," the Earl said again. "So permit me to make the position clear to myself. You are afraid that the stiff-necked Reeds may learn that Peregrine has been cutting a dash in town on my money and refuse consent to Charlotte's marriage with him, especially, I collect, as you expect me at any moment to call in Peregrine's bills and allow the duns to hound him. And only let Sir Stannard catch a whiff of such scandalous possibilities, and our gallant baronet would take to his heels and your family would lose their entrancing prospects, would they not?"

Georgina felt sick with impotent rage. "I see nothing wrong in being concerned for my loved ones' happiness, sir, although I would expect you to sneer."

"But naturally." He gave a small bow. "You appear able to predict with astonishing accuracy my every response."

For a moment she was silent then she said in low tones, "There is no need for you to distress my family. I am here to . . . to offer . . . myself . . . in payment of our debts."

He drew in a sharp breath, and his eyes narrowed. "So! You capitulate. Allow me to itemise what you offer, as I wish to be perfectly clear.

"For the sake of your dear ones you are prepared to lay

yourself upon the altar of matrimony—to sublimate your independence and your designs for your future and assume the role of meek and obedient wife. To take me as a husband— and all that goes with me, of course. We must not forget the position as Countess, a great deal of money, a few trifling baubles of jewels and the rest. I need not go into complete detail now. Later will be a sufficient time to acquaint you with what you have gained."

His scorn lashed her, but she continued to speak quietly. "Once more you do not read me aright. I offer you my person. I will not tie myself to you in a loveless marriage."

This time the silence seemed interminable, and Georgina felt her nerves grow taut. She heard the steady *clip-clopping* of a horse's hooves and the rumble of light carriage wheels which seemed to stop at the front door.

The Earl strolled to the window and said, dispassionately, "They have brought my curricle, I see. I ordered it for an earlier time. Such laxity. I fear I must give the stables a roasting—perhaps make some changes there."

Georgina began to shake and picking up her wine, sipped it in an attempt to steady herself as, still gazing outside, the Earl continued in exactly the same tones, "If you take the course you propose, will not your departure from London at the height of the Season cause comment? If a scandal reaches the ears of the town, there will certainly be no marriages for your sister and brother.

"Ah! But I think I comprehend. You do not despise me sufficiently to fear that I will blazen your shame to the world. I think we must devise for you a sudden illness which necessitates your immediate removal to a quiet place in the country. I feel convinced that once your loved ones understand that your reputation is irretrievably ruined they will be only too glad to fall in with my plan for secrecy."

He strolled to the fireplace and gave the bell rope a tug and when the butler appeared said, "Tell them to return my curricle to the stable and to prepare with all haste my post-chaise and pair. I am going on a journey."

He turned to Georgina and said in a voice completely lacking expression, "I accept your offer, Miss Havard. Pray excuse me. There are arrangements I must make. First I have to ask you if you have disclosed your plan to anyone."

"I was angry," confessed Georgina stonily. "I spoke in haste, and Lady Dorothea knows."

"Good God, does she though? We shall need to make our escape with all speed. Where was she when you departed?"

"I locked her in my bed-chamber. The door is thick, so she may not be heard for a while, though when I ran away she sounded very cross."

There was a choking sound from Lord Rivington, and Georgina looked sharply at him. But his face was composed as he left the room. Georgina continued to sit where he had left her. She picked up a leather-bound book which had been lying open on the small table beside her and put it down again without seeing the words. Her hot rage had died, leaving her coldly miserable.

"I must be mad," she told herself. There was still time to escape. She half rose from her chair, feeling that she could not continue on such a course. Then Lord Rivington's words seemed to echo through her brain—"your brother in a debtors' gaol." She visualised what could happen should the town discover that the Havards were not only penniless but deep in debt and sank back, closing her eyes. What madness had allowed her to offer herself without marriage? She knew that many ton weddings were not graced by love. What difference could it have made if hers had joined the others? Then she clasped her hands. She would not, could not, forgo the principles by which she had vowed to govern her life. She would not marry for convenience.

The thought came unbidden that it was already too late for her. Lord Rivington, that harsh, uncompromising man, would no longer consider marriage since he now knew he could take her without it. And to her grief and shame, she felt a great tide of anguished disappointment wash over her. She realised, with a sickening distaste for her own weakness, that she had not expected or wanted him to accept her on her own terms. She had believed, deep within herself, that he would laugh away her offer and demand marriage—and that she would have allowed herself to be persuaded.

She knew that in spite of her beliefs in the emancipation of women she would never be able to kill her love for Alexander Rivington, and fear of the future came and sat like a spectre on her shoulder.

CHAPTER 11

Georgina was startled by a gentle cough from the doorway and looked up to see a tall, thin man, dressed in black.

He coughed again behind a slender hand. "Excuse me, madam. I am Digweed, his lordship's valet. His lordship has sent me to enquire if there is anything you desire. His lordship expresses his apologies for the delay, but there are certain notes he must send to friends. We are, I collect, to take a journey. Naturally his lordship has engagements he must cancel."

"Of . . . of course," stammered Georgina. "No, there is nothing I need, I thank you."

Even as she spoke she suddenly realised that in her haste she had rushed out of the house without a stitch save what she wore. How did one set about asking a comparative stranger to purchase essential garments for her? She could not possibly go back.

A flush stained her pale face, but Digweed remained professionally devoid of expression as he glided from the room.

Georgina bit her lip fiercely. She had not considered the peering eyes and knowing leers of servants. Yet why should not Lord Rivington take Digweed with him? An escapade like this could be no new thing for either of them, she reflected bitterly, and it was probably a regular part of the valet's duties to superintend such arrangements.

The Earl entered the room as a commotion erupted at the front door. His brows rose haughtily as his butler said loudly, "We do not admit tradespeople here, my girl. Round to the back with you this instant."

A female voice shrilled above his. "I will not go away. I know my young lady to be here, and see her I must and will."

Georgina started to her feet. "It is Jenny—my maidservant. But how . . . ?"

The door was thrust violently open, and Jenny darted through, followed by a red-faced butler who stopped at the sight of his master. "My lord," he panted, forgetting in his agitation to bow, "this . . . this person pushed me aside. I could not restrain her."

"Evidently," remarked the Earl. He waved his man away and lifted his quizzing glass to contemplate Jenny, who stood ground valiantly, then gave a small curtsey. "I beg your lordship's pardon for my rude behaviour, but I have brought some necessaries for my young lady. She cannot travel without . . . certain items . . . and where she goes I go."

"Good heavens!" cried Georgina, "does all the world know what I am about?"

Jenny turned swiftly to her. "No, indeed, miss, but I heard such a banging and a shrieking from your bed-chamber I thought at least you must be attacked by miscreants, and when I unlocked the door, I was almost trampled by Lady Dorothea. Oh, miss, she was beside herself with fury. I heard her muttering your name and feared some harm had befallen you."

Here she stopped and stared at her feet, her face flushing.

"Go on," said Georgina gently.

"Yes, pray do," begged Lord Rivington. "I swear this is better than the play."

Both girls glared at him, and Jenny confessed, "I . . . I followed her ladyship to the drawing room, where she found Mrs. Havard and Miss Penelope. I . . . I listened at the door. I do not in a general way behave so, Miss Georgina, please believe me . . ."

Georgina smiled encouragement, and Jenny said, "I heard that you had left to . . . to . . ." She blushed and gave the Earl a sideways glance.

"We will excuse you from finishing the sentence," he said blandly. "What then occurred?"

"Poor Mrs. Havard went into violent hysterics, and Miss Penelope swooned. Lady Lutterworth called me to help attend them. When they began to recover, she left to seek out Mr. Peregrine, but it seems that he has slipped the watchfulness of Bendish and has gone driving to Kew with Miss Ingram.

"I heard no more as I dashed to your bed-chamber then, miss, and—here I am."

"You mentioned—necessaries," said the Earl.

"Yes, sir, I brought a bundle. It is in the hall."

The Earl went into the hall and returned with Jenny's burden, which was wrapped in Georgina's grey velvet, fur-trimmed travelling cloak.

"I knew you would need it, madam, and you will find your matching bonnet also. I do hope it is not crushed."

"I too," agreed the Earl.

Ignoring him, Jenny continued, "There is also your green silk dress, in case the weather should turn warmer as it often does in spring, and a reticule, gloves, slippers and your best white-fur muff. Also . . ." She grabbed the white shawl which Georgina had been about to investigate, and with a glance at the Earl, finished, "There are other items wrapped in here for your convenience, miss."

"Dear me," said the Earl, "this affair becomes bigger by the minute. I take it, young woman, that you do not intend to desert your mistress."

"Never!" declared Jenny.

"Ah, then I will instruct Digweed to engage another post-chaise for you and himself, and you can follow with the baggage. Digweed has our direction. He will no doubt be charmed to travel in greater comfort. Even a hired vehicle will be kinder to him than if he were clinging to my carriage as usual."

He turned to Georgina. "Your cloak, my dear, and your bonnet, which I delight to see is not at all crushed. We really must be going before the pursuit begins."

As she slipped the cloak over her shoulders and stood on tip-toe to peep into the looking glass over the fireplace to adjust her bonnet, Georgina felt an air of unreality creeping over her. This was not how seductions were conducted in romantic novels. The Earl seemed to be acting at times with an air of levity which was very irritating to her nerves and she had to take a deep breath to force herself to reply with cold civility, "I am ready, my lord." As she placed her hand upon the arm held out for it, her eyes met his. An expression flickered in the grey depths for a moment. It was gone before she could analyse it, and his face resumed its customary cynical demeanor.

The Earl inspected his pair of splendid bay horses, nodded approval, and gave a murmured command to the postillion before handing Georgina into the waiting chaise and climbing in after her. A waiting footman put up the steps and closed the door; the postillion took his position on the near-side animal, and the journey began.

"I trust you are quite comfortable, Georgina. I may call you that now, may I not, since we are to become more closely acquainted?"

Georgina almost ground her teeth. How could he sound so placid? It could come only from long practise at this sort of escapade. She felt a bewildering mixture of emotions, of which embarrassment was one of the uppermost. Yet she had offered herself, and she presumed she must now make some effort to appear composed.

"Very comfortable, my lord. The chaise is so well-sprung and the squabs so . . . so yielding."

"The colour too, dear Georgina. Do not forget the colour. I delight in the richness of the red Morocco. I little knew when I chose it how enchanting a background it would make to your charms. And your maid could hardly have picked a cloak which contrasted better, though if you should wish to remove your cloak, the shade of your gown would not appear to such advantage. But we will not distress ourselves with unimportant details now. Later, when you are properly established, you may make whatever changes suit you."

Georgina forced herself to look straight into his face. Was he taunting her? She could not tell. He met her look with a bland smile which did not reach his eyes and conveyed nothing.

She felt unable to continue the conversation and relapsed into silence, staring from the chaise window as the streets of London gave way to fields and woods. She had no idea where she was being taken, but she supposed that the Earl must have a discreet residence to which he could retire in such circumstances. She wondered if they would travel far and decided they would not. He would surely wish to keep the scene of his *amours* within a convenient distance of town, and if he had been committed to a long journey, he would have used four horses and not two.

Consequently she was surprised as the horses drew into an inn yard, and Lord Rivington climbed out and offered her his arm to descend.

"Why so, my lord?" she asked coldly. "I would prefer to stay where I am. I do not wish to be recognised so near London."

"Pull your cloak up to hide your face if you so desire,"

was the urbane reply, "though I do not think we shall meet anyone of consequence here. We have a journey before us, and it will be some while before we eat, so we will take refreshment here, at the Old Hatte Inn, while the postillion takes the horses to be changed at the Green Man. I keep my own animals there in readiness at all times, but I feel we shall be sure of greater seclusion here."

Still Georgina delayed. She felt that by entering a public inn with him she was committing herself irrevocably to her present course. What would happen, she wondered, if she should tell Lord Rivington that she could not continue, but must return home immediately? She found herself giving him a look almost of entreaty. His features were immobile in their sardonic expression; his grey eyes were cold and hard. Forcing herself to remember why she had taken this step, she placed her hand upon his arm and allowed herself to be led into the private parlour of the inn while the chaise and pair went clattering down the highway.

"Digweed and your maid will eat at the Green Man," explained the Earl. "I hope I have not been hasty in arranging this; there is nothing you require of your maid?"

His forehead was creased in a spurious frown. She shook her head and accepted an offer of coffee and bread and butter, while the Earl sat at a table and brought a good appetite to cold meat and bread, which he washed down with wine.

Then they reentered the chaise, drawn now by black horses which stamped and snorted their impatience to be gone and at four o'clock the journey continued. As change followed change and the miles sped away beneath the hooves of high-bred animals, Georgina felt almost numb. The swaying chaise seemed to have been her home forever; the Earl, who had given up any attempt to pierce her unwillingness to talk, leaned against the squabs with his eyes closed. He might have been her companion of years.

At last the chaise turned off the post road and entered a lane which was deeply rutted by cart marks. Now they bounced and swayed as the wheels hit large stones or descended into mud-filled cavities and the postillion was forced to slow to walking pace.

Georgina's heartbeats quickened. This must be the road to their final destination. Suddenly her mouth became dry and she held on tightly to the leather coach strap, clenching a hand inside her muff to hide her shaking. It was seven o'clock by her fob watch when the chaise pulled to a halt and she found to her surprise that she was outside a small, shabby inn. The overhanging trees held out what small light there was and the squat stone building was nothing like what she had expected.

Reading her thoughts accurately, the Earl explained, "We are at the village of Stokinchurch, my dear. It would not be safe for the horses to travel further along so rough a road without a moon, so we will lie here for tonight."

Though small and obviously not patronised by Quality, the inn was clean. Georgina felt thankful to sink into a tolerably comfortable chair near a fire in the small upstairs private parlour where the Earl left her for a moment, returning with the information that dinner would shortly be served.

"I trust that my choice of menu will please you," he said, his brow creasing with exaggerated humility. "We shall eat simply, but appetisingly. The landlord's wife was used to work for me, and I know her to be an excellent cook. I took the liberty of ordering a gravy soup with yellow peas, trout, a duckling and an apricot tart. I sent the apricots with my messenger so as to be sure we would not meet with disappointment.

"If there is any dish which does not have your approval, please do not hesitate to say so, and I will discover what else may be had."

"Really, sir, there is no need to take such trouble. I have not a large appetite . . . the food will suit me very well."

For the past hour she had been feeling hungry, but although the dishes looked and smelled appetising, she found her stomach rebelled, and she ate almost nothing.

During the meal they heard the bustle announcing the arrival of Jenny and Digweed, and the fat landlady hurried to give instructions regarding the baggage, leaving her equally plump husband to serve.

Georgina had searched the faces of the couple, but had found nothing but polite regard written on both. The woman was his former servant, and Georgina wondered if this was why she allowed Lord Rivington to use the inn for his base purposes. No doubt he paid them well; possibly he even owned the inn.

After dinner, the events of the day began to take their toll and Georgina felt unbearably tired. She longed hopelessly for her own quiet room and chaste bed. Again the air of unreality possessed her. Were all seductions like this? Did such flights usually end with the man blandly accepting what the lady had to offer while she tried to control increasing weariness from a long, jolting journey?

The Earl broke in upon her thoughts. "You ate scarcely a thing. Are you not hungry?"

If he had shown any understanding of her feelings at this point, she felt she could have broken down and begged for mercy, but his tone was such that he might have been enquiring directions from a stranger, and she merely answered through stiff lips, "Not very, my lord."

He tapped his long fingers on the table, then said, "My name is Alexander. I should be obliged if you would use it."

She inclined her head. "As you wish."

"Then let me hear you say it."

Almost choking over the word, she stammered, "Alex . . . Alexander."

"I suppose that must satisfy me for now. Do please sit near the fire. I have ordered a light wine to be served you before we retire. I fear you may find it difficult to sleep in the circumstances."

Her face flamed, but he continued calmly, "I have bespoken a private room for you, Georgina."

"But I thought . . ." Her voice trailed away. How could she put into words what her mind still refused to accept.

She watched, fascinated, as Lord Rivington drew from a pocket in his coat tail a small gold snuff box, flicked it open with one finger and delicately took a pinch of snuff from the back of his hand. "You believed, I daresay, that having embarked upon yet another episode of seduction in a life crammed with such affairs, that I would not be able to contain my passion for you.

"You are mistaken. I have no intention of beginning what I hope will prove a pleasant liaison in such surroundings as these. Tomorrow I shall conduct you to more suitable quarters."

Relief flooded her. She knew that the moment of surrender was only being postponed, but that must suffice for now. The landlord bustled in and made a great play of serving her with the wine which she drank gratefully.

Later Jenny helped her to bed, and Georgina could not but be thankful that the faithful girl had followed her with her toilet items. Even in such dubious circumstances, it was comforting to have about one all the small items which made life so ordered; in fact, much more so, she reflected miserably.

The wine lulled her to a sounder sleep than she had expected, and she awoke to find Jenny bringing her coffee and drawing back the window curtains.

"It's a lovely day, miss. I should wear your velvet again, but when we arrive where he's taking us, you'll be able to change into your cooler gown. I . . . I daresay his lordship will purchase other things you will need."

She was making a valiant attempt to keep her voice casual, and Georgina felt a warm affection for her.

She helped her mistress to dress, then packed their meagre luggage into a portmanteau which bore the Rivington crest.

"Mr. Digweed loaned it to us, miss," she explained. "He's

nice and not a bit starchy when you get to know him."

The Earl breakfasted well on beef and ham washed down by ale while Georgina had difficulty eating even a morsel of the freshly baked rolls which were served with butter and quince preserves.

She had not realised that he was paying attention to anything but his food until he said, so abruptly that she started, "You do not eat enough. It is no wonder that you are still too thin. I shall make sure your appetite improves."

She coloured with indignation. If her figure was so displeasing to him, why had he taken the trouble to pretend to be attracted to her—making jibes at her so-called "beauty"? And what right had he to criticise or to plan her future conduct? She opened her mouth to protest, then closed it again. She had given him the right, and it was not now for her to object.

She glanced up at him and saw that he was watching her closely, a look of amusement dancing briefly in his eyes. She suspected that he knew exactly what struggle had just taken place in her mind, and she had to bite her tongue to hold back her indignant reproaches.

Their journey across country continued along paths which in places were little more than farm tracks, and Georgina felt thankful when at last the wheels began to bowl along a more civilised highway and the jolting ceased. She reckoned that they had travelled about ten miles from the inn when the chaise stopped at a pair of enormous iron gates. In answer to a shout from the postillion, they were opened smartly by a woman wearing a checked gingham apron, who dropped a curtsey as they passed.

Now they were on a road as smooth as silk, and the chaise drove between an avenue of stately elm and oak, which was clearly long-established. A turn in direction brought a sight which made Georgina gasp. Sprawled across the landscape was a huge stone dwelling that encompassed periods of building from mediaeval to present day.

The Earl chuckled at her look. "My Berkshire residence," he announced. "Thankfully, I have been able to render it more homelike and comfortable than you would guess from the exterior."

"You cannot be thinking of taking me there! It is not seemly. It would be against all . . . all . . ."

"Pray continue."

He was mocking her again, and she felt like shaking him until the sardonic smile left his face. Then he said softly, "You are so right, Georgina, it would not be seemly. We shall find somewhere more suited to your present position."

The coach branched off onto a minor driveway and descended a long hill at the bottom of which it rounded a bend, revealing a sight which caused Georgina to exclaim in admiration. From behind an ancient stone wall rose the mellow red brickwork of an Elizabethan dwelling. The sun turned the bricks to rose and threw back glinting light from the mullioned windows. A thin curl of blue smoke rose from a chimney.

The Earl was watching her reaction with a smile. "I take it that this meets more with your approval."

"It is truly beautiful."

"An ancestor of mine built it. When the ceremony of their large house began to pall, or when they could be spared from Court, he and his wife were used to repair here, though of course in those days the roads were well nigh impassable save in summer."

"I can well understand them," breathed Georgina. "To think of languishing in the tedium of London when all this loveliness lay within a day's travel—or perhaps two in those days."

A thought struck her, and she looked sharply at him. "In these modern times was it necessary for us to spend a night on the road? And to journey along such excessively bad routes?"

"So eager, my dear Georgina?" He laughed softly as she

turned her flushed face away. "I thought," he continued, "that by using a devious approach we would throw off any pursuit. I had enquiries made this morning and made sure that no one preceeded us here."

His voice and face gave nothing away, and Georgina was forced to accept what he said, though she felt his explanation quite unsatisfactory. No one who knew of their flight would imagine for one instant that he would take her to one of his family residences.

The chaise bowled through open gates, up a short curved drive from which Georgina could see the neatly laid out walks and clipped hedges so favoured by the Elizabethans, and drew up before a heavy oak door which was opened at once. An elderly woman appeared and made her way with difficulty down the half-dozen stone steps to the drive and hobbled to them as fast as her crippled state would allow. Her face creased with a delighted smile as the Earl stepped down, and she seized one of his hands and planted a smacking kiss upon it.

"Welcome, Lord Alexander, welcome indeed. Where is she? Where is the young lady? We are all agog."

Lord Rivington handed Georgina to the drive, and the woman bobbed her a curtsey, giving her a penetrating look. "*Mmm,* not exactly pretty, but decidedly winsome and a face full of character. You have made a nice choice, I think."

The Earl laughed and turned to Georgina. "This forward dame is Mrs. Curling, once my nurse and now my housekeeper and very good friend. She abuses her past power over me by behaving in a disgracefully familiar fashion. I beg you will excuse her."

Georgina gave the old lady a tremulous smile and thanked her for her welcome, but she felt bewildered· The woman looked to be highly respectable. How could she countenance the libertine behaviour of her former charge? Georgina must assume that she was so besotted with admiration for her beloved Lord Alexander that all that he did was right in her eyes.

The hall was oak-panelled and gently warmed by the heaped red ash in the open grate. The smell of woodsmoke tickled Georgina's nostrils and mingled sweetly with the scent of lavender and beeswax with which the carved oak chests and chairs had been frequently polished. On one of the low, deep windowsills stood a sturdy brown earthenware vase filled with bluebells. They made a splash of brilliant colour against the leaded panes.

Georgina drew a deep breath. "This is beyond anything lovely. Is all the house the same?"

Lord Rivington smiled. "All except the kitchen, which I have had improved by the addition of a modern stove. I see no reason to make servants work harder than necessary, though," grinning at Mrs. Curling, "this stubborn old woman still prefers to use the old fire stove as often as not."

Mrs. Curling chuckled as he continued, "Please be so kind as to direct Miss Havard to her room and send her maid to her. I think I hear the second chaise in the distance."

"Of course, sir. This way, Miss Havard. Lord Alexander's messenger told us last night to expect you today, and all is in readiness."

She led the way up stairs which were uncarpeted and worn with the tread of many feet and showed Georgina into a bed-chamber overlooking the front gardens. "I'll leave you now, miss, and find your maid. Should you like some tea sent up?"

"Yes . . . yes, thank you. That would be most refreshing."

Mrs. Curling bobbed a curtsey and left. Georgina looked around her. The uneven oak floor was mostly concealed by a velvety Brussels carpet of softly mingled shades of deep red and gold. A rosewood commode awaited her possessions, and a delicate Sheraton writing table sat near the window. Beside the crested writing paper, inkstand, and quills, someone had placed a small jug of creamy jade containing sweet violets. Georgina walked past the bed, with its lovely hand-embroidered hangings and quilt in shades which blended with the carpet, and smelled the flowers. Their exquisite scent reminded her of the damp spring woods at home, where she knew a sudden passionate longing to be.

She jerked her mind from such weakness. She had gone too far now to withdraw. By staying alone last night at an inn with Lord Rivington she had destroyed her reputation and she had as well continue this hateful masquerade now. She would have the name and might as well pay the piper who had made them dance to his tune, she reflected bitterly.

Jenny arrived with the tea, her eyes popping with excitement. At first Georgina found it difficult to understand her meaning, but when she did she felt nausea rise and choke her.

"She's downstairs now," bubbled Jenny, "my friend—you know, the one you saw in Hyde Park that day you gave me my position. Queeney—with the baby."

"Downstairs!"

"Yes, miss. This is where he brought her and her child. She lives here she says, with the babe, and is very happy, having as she tells me a kind mistress and you'll never conceive who . . ."

"Be silent!"

Jenny's mouth fell open. Never had she imagined that her beloved lady could have spoken to her so harshly.

"Please, leave me. Now!"

Jenny scurried from the room leaving Georgina pacing up and down, alternately wringing her hands and muttering angry words of despair. He had brought her here, to the same place as his former mistress. They were to share the same roof. How dare he! How could he! Then she sank into a chair, her hands over her face. So that was how he regarded her. Once or twice, just briefly, she had dared to imagine, to hope that he looked upon her in a special kind of way. His easy acceptance of her sacrifice had left her with her illusions sadly impaired.

Now there could be no more room for self-deception. She was not of any particular value to him. She was simply one of a succession of women who would amuse him, distract his boredom for a while, then be discarded. He had taken in Jenny's friend because of the child, or maybe because he disliked the idea of notoriety, otherwise she too would have been simply cast aside and left alone.

She stood up abruptly and walked to the washstand to bathe her face in cold water. Then she rang for Jenny, and having requested she assist her to change into the green silk dress and to unpack the portmanteau, she forbade any further speech between them. She ignored the jewel case her maid held out to her. She might be forced to wear his clothes; she was not obliged to wear his jewels. She took a last glance in the cheval glass. The dress was cut in Grecian style and fell in folds about her slender form to her ankles. Her white kid shoes had green bows to match. The outfit suited her to perfection, the colour of the dress giving luminosity to her pale skin and enhancing the green in her hazel eyes which glittered with suppressed anger. She drew a gauzy scarf of a paler hue around her shoulders, allowed Jenny to brush her short curls, then left the room and descended the stairs.

The Earl, who was awaiting her in the hall, was dressed in cream buckskin breeches and a brown cloth coat with brass buttons. A white cravat was loosely knotted about his throat, and he looked far less formal than she had ever seen him, and in Georgina's eyes, infinitely more attractive.

He bowed. "Your maid chose well when she picked that gown, my dear. Be pleased to accompany me. There is someone I would like you to meet."

If he noticed the coldness of her expression and the fury in her eyes, he gave no sign, but drawing her hand to his arm, led her outside. They passed expertly pruned rose bushes which promised well for the summer; flower beds tended so that not a weed was to be seen, and finally walked through a trellis-covered archway into a walled garden at the back of the house.

Here were rows of vegetables of all kinds, and a greenhouse stood in the sunniest spot. A woman was kneeling on a mat, her hands encased in gauntlets, while she dug holes for seedlings which she removed from a box held by a tall, broad-shouldered negro. She rose as she heard their steps. Her simply cut dress was of lavender-sprigged chintz, and a large apron of blue home-spun was tied about her waist. Her snowy lace cap had slipped a little, allowing tendrils of soft white curls to fall over her forehead. She smiled at their approach, and Georgina thought she had never before seen a face of such sweetness and charm.

Georgina was at a loss to know who she might be, especially when Lord Rivington gave her a courtly bow before kissing her hand and then her cheek. At his next words Georgina's heart seemed to contract.

"Mama, please allow me to present Miss Georgina Havard, of whom I have told you.

"Georgina, I am so happy to present you to Lady Elinor, Countess of Rivington—and my dearest Mama."

CHAPTER  Georgina rallied her wits enough to make her curtsey while Lady Elinor drew off her gloves and handed them to the smiling Negro, then put out her dainty hands to clasp Georgina's.

Drawing her near, she kissed her softly. "You will permit a grateful mother's caress, my dear. This is such a happy day for me. To meet with my son's affianced wife at last and to find her so charming and unspoiled. He has told me so much of you."

She turned to the Earl. "Away with you. This is a time when a male's company is superfluous, do you not agree, Georgina?"

Georgina gave a strangled reply as Lord Rivington strode away, and she could have sworn she heard him chuckle.

The Countess put her gloves back on. "Do excuse me for a moment, dear, if I finish planting this bed of heartsease. The poor blooms will wilt, and I hate to leave a task when once I have begun."

"I too," agreed Georgina, "but pray, will you not allow me to help you?"

Apart from not wanting to stand idle while this elderly lady knelt in the dirt, she felt she needed something constructive on which to fasten her mind till she regained control over her whirling thoughts. What did this mean? Was it Lord Rivington's final mockery? Yet the lady at her feet was unquestionably real and too transparently honest surely to partake of a despicable deception.

She had almost forgotten her question when Lady Elinor shook her head. "I cannot allow you to soil yourself today. You are not suitably dressed. But I apprehend that you are not a girl to waste her time in uesless occupations, and we shall, I doubt not, spend many happy hours together in the future."

She finished pressing the soil around the last plant and allowed her servant to help her to her feet, handing him her gloves and trowel before beginning to stroll round the garden with Georgina.

"Ebenezer will water the roots for me. He too dotes on gardening. My husband bought him many years ago, when he was a very young child, to be my slave. It was used to be the fashion to keep a little negro as a kind of lapdog. But I always hated the practice and freed him as soon as I was able. He was stolen from his mother and I offered him the chance to return to his own country to search out his tribe. But I fear it would have been a hopeless task and he thought so too. Also we had grown fond of one another and he decided to stay with me and be a servant, but a free man and my very good friend."

Georgina still felt incapable of coherent speech, but Lady Rivington did not seem to mind. "Alexander's old nurse, dear Mrs. Curling, is another who has been a rock in times of distress. Those two helped to cushion me against despair when I was grievously in need. You may have heard something of my story. I think it a good thing that you are not too conventional a girl or you might not care to acknowledge such a mother as myself, about whom there has been gossip in the past."

"Oh, Lady Elinor, do not say so. I would delight in having you for my Mama—I know I would."

"But you are going to, so that is all right. If Alexander loves you, then I know you must be a very good sort of person. One day I will tell you of his care for me and you will know, even more than you must do now, what a wonderful man he is.

"I believe many find him proud and aloof, but that is because as a child he was forbidden to show his feelings. You and I know what tenderness lies beneath that cool exterior, do we not?"

She fell into a reverie, and Georgina walked silently beside her. She longed to escape to her room to think. Lord Rivington, it now seemed, had never had the least intention of seducing her. He had sent word to his mother that he was bringing his future wife, and all the rest had been simply to amuse himself.

Lady Elinor sat on a carved wood bench and patted it in an invitation to Georgina to join her. "Here is my herb garden." She leaned forward to pluck several leaves and squeeze them between her fingers. "Are not the scents delightful? Fennel, sage, rosemary, yet of them all, I often think the sweet mint the most delicious fragrance.

"Alexander has told me of your care for the sick, so you will recognise some of my rarer medicinal plants. I also am reckoned to have some skill in healing. Perhaps you would be interested in helping me prepare a tea of poplar bark, of which I have recently learned, and which might help poor Mrs. Curling's rheumatism. And I have been longing for someone to discuss with me the possible use of digitalis as a relief for the symptoms of measles. So many of the little ones die or are maimed by this disease.

"A lot of the villagers prefer me to the local physician, especially the women." She chuckled infectiously. "The true reason may be because I make no charge upon their purses."

Georgina laughed with her. There was no mockery here. Then her laughter died as her position became abruptly clear. She would be married to the man she knew she loved deeply; she would have gentle Lady Elinor for her mama, yet all would be false. She could never tell her the truth of what had happened, and worse, she would never now be able to make Alexander believe in her love for him. Whatever she said would be taken for gratitude or mistaken conventionality.

She considered denying the betrothal and begging Lady Elinor for a conveyance back to town, but her courage failed her when she looked at her companion. The Countess was gazing at her herbs pensively, and Georgina could now see the tiny lines which past suffering had etched into her face. She could not destroy the sweet lady's happiness so brutally, and if she was strictly honest with herself, she could not face the contempt which surely Lady Elinor would feel for her should she learn the truth. She believed in her son's love for Georgina and would surely despise any woman who set out to hurt him.

Georgina stared at the patch of fragrant plants, and tears blurred their image. Starved all her life of true maternal affection she sensed the beginning of a new sweet relationship. She would fight no more, but would accept what was offered: love from her husband's mother and from the son as much affection as he was capable of giving. She believed Lady Elinor to be deceived about Alexander's capacity for love, which she was sure had been irreparably impaired long ago. Her heart almost failed her as she contemplated the life ahead of her; the years when she would be driven to hide her passion for her husband because of his innate coldness, but she could see no honourable way out of the tangle.

"If you please, my lady . . ."

A gentle voice broke in on their musings. Georgina had heard no one approaching and was startled to see Queeney standing before them. "Mrs. Curling says, ma'am, that she desires your opinion regarding the herrings which Mr. Digweed brought from London. He says they're fresh, but cook's none too sure of it."

Lady Rivington laughed. "Please excuse me, dear. Do stay and sit a while in the sun if you wish. Cook will serve luncheon shortly. I hope you are hungry. She has made some cheesecakes, of which she is inordinately proud."

As Georgina watched her walk away, talking animatedly to the maid, she felt her resentment returning. She had momentarily forgotten Queeney. How had his lordship persuaded his mother to care for his discarded mistress? Had he lied to her, or was she, like the rest of this household, so enamoured of him as to accept anything he did? She had nearly fallen into the same trap of delusion. Well, she saw no way out of marrying him now, but she would not be won over so easily.

Hearing a step upon the path, she turned to see Lord Rivington striding toward her. Against her will, her heart swelled with the longing she felt for him. For a brief instant she wished she could begin all over again and be wooed and won by him in a straightforward manner. If he had been honest with her, she felt she could have forgiven him much—

even perhaps Queeney. There were excuses to be found, after all, for men who behaved so, when they had been led since boyhood to believe that to seduce a woman was a triumph rather than a sin.

Her lips almost began to tremble in a smile before she realised that his eyes were cool. "Charming as you look, my dear, your appearance would be improved by the addition of this."

He held out his hand and allowed a slender gold chain to slip through his long fingers until the opal swung slowly to and fro, the deep fires within flashing as they caught the sun. His harsh tones brought instant resentment.

"I am not to be compelled to wear your jewellery, sir!"

"You are inconsistent, Georgina. For one who prides herself upon the logic of her mind, as I feel you must do if you believe yourself worthy to be a physician, you must have quite a struggle to bring yourself to wear my clothes, yet refuse my jewels."

"It is not the same . . . !"

"Is it not? I fail to see the subtle difference. You must advise me."

"You are being deliberately obtuse, sir. You must know that I cannot appear without garments."

The Earl smiled, and Georgina flushed as he continued, "See how the opal shows its hidden depths of fire. I chose it with you in mind, of course. Like you, it can look pale, almost without attraction, till it is touched by something which brings it meaning. Then it springs to astonishing life."

"You chose it!"

"But of course Lady Dorothea was instructed in all her actions toward you—and your family—by me."

She did not miss the meaning behind his words. They were all she needed to remind her that but for him Peregrine might even now be lying in a debtors' gaol and her mother and sister heaven knew where. Certainly there would be no anticipation of two splendid weddings in the family—if she submitted to Lord Rivington's commands. And now there would be a third—her own to this domineering man. And he could still destroy her family's hopes. Everything depended on her.

She felt the colour flame her cheeks. Would their whole life together be a constant torment of battles of wills such as these? Was that what he hoped for? It would be wiser to give way before him, yet she could not take the necklace—would not . . .

"Rise, Georgina," he ordered coldly.

She opened her mouth to refuse, but as her eyes met his she found herself drowning in the power which lay in their depths. Dear God, she thought, am I then to become as the women I despise? A wife owned as his own mother had been owned? Had he learned nothing from Lady Elinor's experiences?

Shaking now, she rose to her feet. He made no further attempt to hand her the chain but walked behind her and with firm fingers fastened it at her neck. She felt the coldness of the opal on her breast even as his hand caressed her shoulder briefly.

"Now, my dear, my Mama suggests we join her for nuncheon."

The rest of the day took on the now-familiar dreamlike quality. Lady Elinor and Alexander gossiped happily of mutual acquaintances, pausing often to explain points to Georgina, until the Earl left to interview his Steward, leaving Georgina with his mother, who led her to the airy kitchen where the Countess and a fat cook squabbled amicably over the relative merits of Solid or Whip Syllabub. The matter was settled when Lady Elinor reminded Cook that Lord Alexander preferred the Whip method.

I believe they would allow him to trample them into the ground if they thought it would make him happy, Georgina thought angrily. She sat at the scrubbed table, sipping homemade mead and watching Lady Elinor rubbing loaf sugar over the lemon skins. She remembered suddenly the words of Sir Francis Calland. He had told her that Lord Rivington hid his mother away because he was ashamed of her and kept her so short of money that she was forced to work at menial tasks. The obvious truth was that he adored his mother and that she found a haven here in the everyday round which filled her quiet life. It was so easy, she reflected, to tell the truth in a way which represented it as falsehood.

Sitting there in the kitchen, filled now with appetising smells of the evening meal, the two women busy about their chosen jobs, she felt an uneasiness which tormented her; an anxiety which made her long for solitude. She rose so abruptly as to make Lady Elinor and the cook look round in surprise.

"I find it a little . . . warm," she said haltingly. "Pray excuse me, Lady Elinor. I should so like to walk in your beautiful garden once more."

Her silk gown was ineffective protection against the chill of early evening, and she shivered. It would be more sheltered in the walled enclosure at the back. She would sit there and try to bring some order to her chaotic thoughts.

The mellow brick walls still held some warmth from the sun and she sank thankfully onto the carved bench. The memory of Sir Francis had stirred other recollections. She was tantalised by the feeling that somehow she had misread the actions of those about her. That if only she could think objectively, she would find a key to unlock some mystery. Had Sir Francis deliberately lied to her? Maybe not. A man of his kind would never believe that a woman of Lady Elinor's birth could stoop to enjoy the servile side of domestic life; therefore to him it followed that she must be forced to work as she did.

She heard the scuff of a footstep on the red brick path and saw Queeney who hurried towards her, a worried frown creasing her brow.

"Excuse me for troubling you, miss, but have you seen a

man hereabouts? Looking from my bed-chamber window, I could have sworn . . . I was sure I saw someone I remembered. By the time I had put baby down and reached the garden, there was no sign of him."

"I saw no one," said Georgina. The antagonism which she instinctively felt toward this girl coloured her voice, but Queeney appeared not to notice.

She stood nibbling at her knuckles, and Georgina said, "If you believe that there may be someone here who would harm you then you must inform Lord Rivington on his return. I daresay you were deceived. At this time of evening every moving shadow can appear as a lurking figure. I expect you are of a nervous disposition."

Queeney sighed. "Yes, that's what it is. Yes, you must be right—he would not dare."

She scurried away, and a moment later Georgina heard footsteps which she recognised as Lord Rivington's. At first she would not look in his direction, but fearing how he would interpret her reluctance, she slowly turned her head.

The next minutes were a blur of horror. He was a few paces from the trellised entrance when one of the deepening shadows near the wall seemed to move. There was a flash, a loud report which echoed round the walls of the garden, as a female voice screamed, "No, no, you shall not!" and the Earl fell heavily to the ground and lay still.

Georgina ran on legs which seemed attached to leaden weights and fell on her knees beside the motionless body. From a long way off she heard the shouts of men and the cries of women as she stared into Lord Rivington's pallid face. Blood flowed from a head wound. She moaned, "Please, God, don't let him be dead."

Gently she raised his head and pillowed it on her lap as someone else knelt beside them, and she saw Lady Elinor whose face was as white as her son's. The Countess put her ear to his breast. "His heart is beating quite strongly. Thank you, Queeney," she said as the maid handed her mistress a cloth, with which she gently wiped the wound. She examined it closely.

"I think it is superficial," she announced. "He is stunned, but not, I believe, badly hurt. We must get him inside, and you shall help me to care for him, Georgina. We will decide if it is necessary to call in a physician. I think, though, that between us we are well qualified to care for him."

Even in her distress Georgina recognised that the Countess was talking to help her over the shock, and she looked up gratefully. "I . . . I believe you are right, dear Lady Elinor. I am sorry I am so useless. It was such a terrible thing . . . I saw it happen. Where is the person . . . the wicked one who did this?"

Lady Elinor had been busy bathing the wound from a bowl of water fetched by Queeney. Georgina still held the Earl's head between trembling hands. "He has been apprehended. Ebenezer has locked him in an out-house and now he comes to help I see," she answered.

The negro picked up the Earl as if he had been a featherweight and carried him indoors to lie him carefully on a sofa. Lady Elinor covered him with a blanket and went to fetch lotions and bandages, telling Georgina to stay and keep watch.

She knelt by his side, holding both his cold hands in hers, staring into his face. The danger through which he had passed had emphasised her deep love for him. Would she never be able to tell him how she felt? In unconsciousness the harsh lines were smoothed away, and he looked unbearably vulnerable. She leaned closer to him until she felt his soft breath on her lips. Then she kissed him gently. Her voice was little more than a sigh. "Alexander, my love, my dear one, I love you so. I need you—stay with me. Never leave me."

Moments later, beneath the ministrations of his mother assisted by a fluttering Queeney, the Earl's dark lashes moved and he opened his eyes.

"What the devil . . . ? Where am I? I was in the garden."

"Quiet, my son. You have been wounded. Not seriously, thank God, but you must rest."

He tried to sit up, but the effort made him wince, and he fell back. "My head!"

"You were shot, Lord Alexander," cried Queeney. "I thought I recognised the man from my window, but I could not find him. I believed I must be mistaken, yet I was uneasy. I followed you and was in time to throw myself at your attacker and force up his arm.

"Oh, sir, my lady, he was sent by his wicked master. I saw him once before. To think that your own kinsman should seek to destroy you!"

Lord Rivington frowned. "My kinsman?" He gave Queeney a searching look, then whistled through his teeth. "So that was it. Where is my attacker now?"

"He is safely locked up," said Lady Elinor serenely. "It was a blessing that you brought Queeney here, my son. She saved your life, then Ebenezer overpowered the man. Ably assisted, I may add, by Cook, who dented one of my best copper pans on his skull. Quite unnecessarily, but she acted with the best of intentions."

Lord Rivington grinned and caught his mother's hand and kissed it.

Georgina felt bewildered. They seemed unnaturally calm, and everyone but she seemed to know exactly what had happened.

"Do you know who did this awful thing?" she demanded.

Queeney spoke excitedly. "It was *him,* miss, don't you see? *He* sent him." Queeney's eyes were bright with anger and her face was flushed. "And to think I once loved him and bore that little innocent upstairs for his sake. Pray God he doesn't turn out to be like his father."

"Will somebody please explain," begged Georgina, but a horrible suspicion was forming in her mind. The key for which she had earlier searched was being given her, and it was almost without surprise that she heard Lady Elinor say, "Our kinsman, Sir Francis Calland, sent his man to kill my son."

Georgina knew that the Earl was watching her. Sir Francis Calland had tried to kill Alexander. He was the father of Queeney's child. Bravely she looked full into the Earl's grey eyes and found them warmly sympathetic, then Lady Elinor said briskly, "Bed for you, my boy, at once."

Ebenezer and Digweed carried him upstairs and took him into his bed-chamber, while Lady Elinor led the now-weeping Queeney to the kitchen to give her a restorative, and Georgina was left alone. She sank on to the sofa, still warm from the Earl's body, and stared at the dark stain on her gown. She touched it with a gentle finger and shuddered as she realised how close to death he had been. She had believed before that she had loved him. Now she knew that her love was rooted in the depths of her being and she wanted to go to his side and speak the words of passion and relief which filled her. And she could not.

Lady Rivington entered, and Georgina turned swiftly to her. "Why did Sir Francis want to kill Alexnader? Why should he? Surely he could not be so wicked! And is he not afraid of the consequences?"

The Countess sighed. "Revenge is a motive one would expect from Francis. Alexander has thwarted all his plans for making a wealthy marriage. And do not forget that if my son had died, Francis would inherit the Earldom and all that goes with it. He has always been jealous. At first Alexander tried to give him a part in running and sharing the estates, but his cousin's bad nature caused the scheme to fail. He was dishonest and ruthless toward our tenants. Considerable sums disappeared into his pockets.

"It is all hard for me to accept. His mother was my sister's child and one of my few friends—and I saw him grow up."

"I see. And you said that Alexander prevented Sir Francis

from making a wealthy marriage. How and why . . . ?

Lady Elinor put out her hand. "My son will explain later, my dear. And enough of the past for the time. The future is what should be concerning us. The danger is over and no lasting harm done."

She touched Georgina's shoulder gently. "This has been shocking for you. Go to your room, dear, where your maid is waiting to help you change your gown. This one is ruined, I fear. Such a shame. It is so pretty."

A sob escaped Georgina as she caught at the gentle hand, trying, without success, to speak. The older woman said softly, "I know, my dear. I do understand. Go and change and you shall see him."

You do not understand, Georgina longed to cry. How could you, when I have been such a fool?

Jenny had refurbished the velvet, and after she had changed she stood before the cheval glass staring at the cinnamon folds. Was it only two days ago she had dressed in expectation of an ordinary day? It seemed so much longer. Then she deliberately called for the necklace of orange garnets and eardrops.

Lord Rivington was not in bed as she had expected, but resting on a couch pulled close to the wood fire. He was wearing a dressing gown of deep red and with his saturnine face looked, thought Georgina, like the pictures she had seen of Eastern princes. A white bandage was tied around his head, and he was still very pale.

She put out her hands as he made an attempt to rise. "Do not, I beg you, my lord. You must rest."

"So formal? I thought we had agreed I was to be Alexander."

"Yes, I am sorry. Alexander then."

He motioned her to take a chair beside him. Georgina felt sick from the effort of keeping back the words she ached to speak. It was fast becoming beyond her powers to maintain trivial conversation with him.

She drew a deep breath. "You should be in your bed, I think."

"I hoped you would come. I preferred to receive you here."

"Nevertheless, I believe I should allow you to retire. I will come back tomorrow."

"Is my company then so difficult for you to bear?"

"No—no, not that—I have so much to say, so many questions, I am afraid I will make you ill. Tomorrow will be soon enough."

Her hands were tightly clenched in her lap, and he put out one of his and held them both in his strong, slender fingers. "Georgina, lately I have so regretted the way in which we began our acquaintance. I owe you so much in explanations and apologies."

"And I have been too quick to form wrong conclusions. I . . . I believed you responsible for Queeney's betrayal."

"That was not to be wondered at after the incident in Hyde Park. She claimed my help as a kinsman of Francis and head of his family. Her choice of words before you was unfortunate, but I allowed you to continue in your error when I could have set you right. I was angry that you thought me capable of such behaviour, yet I must admit I gave you no reason to think well of me. I could have explained, for instance, the speed with which I accepted Queeney's claim, which can only have added to your suspicions, but after she had produced a likeness of his mother— it was of no value, being a cheap copy of a miniature—but bearing words in Francis's hand declaring his undying love for Queeney, I could not doubt her credibility. It was unlike Francis to commit himself so definitely. She must have needed a deal of persuasion, poor girl."

He seemed determined to undermine Georgina's resolution to keep full control of her emotions, and she wrenched her thoughts back to Peregrine's injuries at the same hand which now held hers.

"There . . . there is still the matter of my brother," she faltered. "I do not yet comprehend why you forced a quarrel on him and hurt him so cruelly."

"And do you believe the whole affair was inspired by wanton revenge on my part?"

"How can I know what to think, my lord?"

Slowly he withdrew his hand, and his voice became flat and a little harsh. "One day you may learn to trust me, Georgina. I tell you, it went very much against my nature to injure your brother. Shortly before leaving the club in the early hours of that morning, I discovered that Peregrine was to meet Francis in a duel as soon as dawn broke."

"A duel! But why?"

"Francis wanted your brother out of the way and was so resolved to beat him that I had reason to suspect he was about to use treachery—in plain language, to cheat."

"Does he hate Peregrine so much? I thought they were friends."

"Hates—and fears—him."

"Fears him? But what can Peregrine do to him?"

"He has gained the love of Charlotte Ingram, whom Francis was determined to have for himself. He needs her fortune to pay his crippling debts."

"But killing Peregrine would only have made her loathe him."

"Francis would never let the small matter of a lady's loathing stand in his way. It seems she was indiscreet enough when she refused his latest offer to explain that his suit was useless as she loved Peregrine. Unwittingly she almost brought about your brother's death. I have caused enquiries to be made which show that Francis was about to abduct Charlotte and force her to accompany him abroad, where shame at her lost reputation would have ensured their marriage. It was not so difficult to discover what I needed to know." The Earl's lip curled. "My kinsman employs those who would sell their souls for gold."

"He is despicable! But even so, he could have carried out his plan without destroying Perry."

"And what think you your brother would have done when he heard that Charlotte had been violated by Francis?"

Georgina spoke slowly. "He would never have rested till he found her. He would have avenged her by slaying Francis in any way he could, then spent the rest of his life making her forget her misery."

"And Francis read his character aright. He knew he must get Peregrine out of the way, so he chose a duel he would win. He would have had to leave the country, of course, for killing his man, but he intended doing so anyway with Charlotte. Later, when the scandal died, he would have returned, complete master of her large fortune."

"And I believed Sir Francis to be his friend!" cried Georgina. "I thought that Perry would be safe with an older man to guide him. He is despicable!"

The Earl continued calmly, "It was necessary for Francis to keep an appearance of friendship to enable him to discover Peregrine's meetings with Charlotte and to further his downfall. He tried, I think, to use you to advance his interests."

Slight colour stained her cheeks. "I had already begun to find his company unwelcome.

"But you spoke of cheating. Surely you must be wrong there. I am sure I have read that identical pistols must be used—that opposing seconds must load and check the firearms and all must be conducted in the prescribed manner. To do otherwise would have made Sir Francis an outcast from society—and the fight might not have taken place at all. I believe that matters of cheating at cards and duelling to be far more serious in the eyes of the Polite World than the mere seduction of a female," she added bitterly.

"I did not formulate the rules," protested the Earl. His tone was mild, but something in his voice impelled Georgina to look sharply into his face.

"You are weary, Alexander. You should rest."

"Later. I must finish now that I have begun. And whether or not Francis cheated would have made no difference to a dead Peregrine. Also, my kinsman would not have been caught. He is not such a fool.

"It would have been contrived that your brother received the pistol designated by Francis. The one he himself was to use has been rifled. That is, the barrel was grooved near the breech end, which causes the bullet to spin with far more accuracy to its target. And the gun barrel had been bored at a slight angle to keep the bullet low. Neither modification is easily detectable and would certainly have been missed by Robert Kennerley and the other inexperienced youth acting as Peregrine's seconds. And to complete the picture for you, Georgina, Francis is a deadly shot."

She shuddered. "Could you not have gone to Wimbledon, proved that Sir Francis was cheating, and stopped the duel?"

"Perhaps I might have tried. But both men were by then determined to fight to the death. They would have met soon after. Francis knows that, for the sake of family honour, I would not have made the matter of the pistol public, and Peregrine was too hot with rage to listen to reason. I have no doubt that within days, maybe hours, your brother would have lain dead.

"My best course seemed to be to attack Francis where it would do most damage—in his purse—and I needed to gain time. By then, I was not the only man to know of the proposed duel. It would have been a simple matter to change the venue at the last moment, and I should have failed to save Peregrine.

"As it was, the news of our bout of fisticuffs was carried to Francis rapidly and he went to ground, having guessed my motives. But I traced him and reminded him that he is dependent on me for his means to live and that a condition of his ever receiving any more money was the safety of your brother.

"I also informed him that Charlotte would be too closely watched in future by those I could trust for him to have the least success in any other base plan he might conceive.

"He knew he was safe from public disgrace at my hands. My mama has had enough to bear in that line, but it all added to the hatred he feels for me."

Sparks flew up as a piece of wood shifted in the grate and Georgina looked down at her twisting hands. "I heard from Charlotte, that the quarrel you forced on Peregrine was on her account. I thought . . ."

Lord Rivington gave a mirthless laugh. "It must all have added up to a pretty picture in your mind, but a false one, my dear. About to fight his first duel over a matter of card play, Peregrine was aggressive. He would not listen to a word from me, and I was compelled to use quite unseemly language about his beloved. I must apologise to him, by the way. It will not do to be on bad terms when we are brothers. And maybe he will take my advice against trusting men like Francis, who employ unscrupulous lures to entice greenhorns into gaming hells. He was determined to reduce you all to a state of poverty which would hasten your departure from London."

"Everything you have done has been for my family."

"Everything I have done has been to ease your life, my wayward Georgina, I made up my mind I would have you and would allow nothing to impede that design."

"Are you always so ruthless?"

"I have never before found it necessary to be so devious. But I wanted you."

"Your mama thinks you care for me."

He did not reply, and suddenly she knew that she could not marry him without telling him the truth about her feelings. She had always prided herself on her honesty and fearlessness and she would not continue with this charade. The knowledge of her love might divert him; it would certainly give him power over her, but that was a risk she must take.

She looked at him and found him watching her intently, his grey eyes alight with amusement—and something else. Her voice was not quite steady as she began, "Lord Rivington—Alexander—I have to tell you . . ."

". . . that you love me. I know, my darling. I was not unconscious all the time. I must apologise for having been obliged to receive your first spontaneous kiss with apparent indifference."

"You were pretending!"

"Not so! I was incapable of physical movement for some while after my senses returned. I was confused, bewildered, stunned, but I knew I was not dreaming when I felt your lips and heard the words I have longed above all others to hear."

"You have longed . . . ? But I thought . . ."

"I know what you thought. We have been at such cross purposes, you and I, and it has been greatly my fault. Can you truly love such a coward as myself, Georgina?"

He stopped her protests with a gentle touch upon her lips. "Oh, not a physical one, but any fool can be careless of his skin. Mine has been a moral weakness; I have been hiding behind a wall of insolence and hauteur because I was afraid of being hurt."

Georgina said nervously, "I have been less than kind, and since this seems to be a moment for confession, can you love someone who was fast becoming a prig?"

"You? Never!"

"Oh, yes, I believe I was," said Georgina quietly. "I have been too ready to think myself always right and to pass judgement on others. I have frequently condemned my Mama and sister for their selfish frivolities while being overly concerned with my own ambitions."

"No, my darling, I will not have it! When you first offered your . . . your person to me, I scarce knew whether to kneel at your feet or to laugh at your idiocy in thinking I would take advantage of you."

As their hands met and clung Lady Elinor entered and

beamed a look of approval. "Please forgive me. I would not have intruded, but I have been talking with the man who shot you, Alexander. His history is grim indeed.

"It seems that about two years ago he was forced from his small farm by the land enclosures and could find no work in town. He was desperate when he stole food for his family and was caught by Francis, who graciously declined to hand him over to the law. Then the poor wretch discovered that the price of freedom was slavery to our dear kinsman, who has forced him into all manner of dishonesty.

"This last act was to be the one which would buy his release forever from threats of transportation or death. He is a pitiful weakling who weeps now at the thought of being torn from his wife and several children. Indeed, he was so shaken by horror and shame, I wonder if he could have fired true enough to kill you, even without Queeney's intervention."

The Earl and his mother studied one another for a while, then both smiled as Alexander said, "The Scottish estates, I think, Mama."

"I hoped you would decide so. I believe he will live an exemplary life, with proper guidance, and serve you well."

"But he tried to murder you," cried Georgina. "I favour mercy with all my heart, but I could not bear that he should try again."

Alexander spoke softly, but his voice was grim. "Without Francis to prod him I shall be safe enough. And my cousin will long since have fled to some Continental country, where he will safely deny all knowledge of an attempt on my life.

"I shall find him and send word that he will receive no more money from me if ever he seeks to return. I shall also inform him that his unhappy former servant is now in my employ and could, no doubt, have an extremely informative talk with a discerning magistrate should I consider such a course to be desirable.

"I have long been aware of Francis's doubtful activities,

and although Mama and I would deplore public scandal, there must be a limit to what we are prepared to endure. I shall tell him so."

"Then that is settled," declared Lady Elinor. "Now I shall leave you to enjoy one another's company. I know that Georgina is too thoughtful and considerate to stay longer than your strength permits, my son. In fact, my future daughter is all I have hoped for."

She bent and kissed Georgina's cheek. "Oh, my dear girl, I look forward with such pleasure to the years to come."

After she had gone there was a short silence, broken by Georgina, who asked hesitantly, "Would you answer one more question, Alexander?"

"Anything, my love."

"That . . . that long jolting journey here—and the stay at the little inn—why was it necessary to create such discomfort? I find I cannot believe your story of pursuit."

The Earl looked quickly into her eyes, his face alight with humour. "I was unable to resist the temptation. I had, of course, written to your family, informing them of our betrothal and your departure to visit my Mama. After your outburst to Lady Dorothea I have no doubt that my letter reposes at this moment in her jewel box, safely under lock and key, as clear evidence of my honourable intent.

"No, my dear, we had no fear of pursuit, but you were so full of fury and dignity, I could not resist the impulse. I swear I was hard put at times to keep my composure."

He choked with mirth, and Georgina felt a flash of the old resentment before her sense of the ridiculous brought a gleam to her eyes and an appreciative laugh.

Then their laughter faded as the Earl pulled her toward him. His arms went about her. Grey eyes met hazel in complete trust and understanding, before their lips joined in their first perfect kiss.

DATE DUE

DEC 14 '76	JE 30 '93		
FEB 8 '77	AG1 0 '98		
MAR 14 '77	AG 0 9 '00		
MAR 28 '77			
MAY 11 '77			
MAY 17 '77			
MAY 27 '77			
JUN 20 '77			
JUL 20 '77			
AUG 17 '77			
OCT 5 '77			
MAY 30 '78			
SEP 22 '78			
OCT 18 '78			
DEC 13 '78			
JUN 4 '79			
MR 29 '91			
AP 0 5 '91			
GAYLORD			PRINTED IN U.S.A.